Praise for *Dogs of Summer*

'Bold, dazzling, hilarious. Andrea Abreu is a lively meteorite in the landscape of Hispanic Literature'

Fernanda Melchor, author of International Booker-shortlisted *Hurricane Season*

'Like the tide. A force of nature. It drags you. It submerges you. And, all of a sudden, it leaves you stranded on a rich and prophetic insular world of women and low, grey, clouds that merge with the sea. It is pure poetry. A book that carries you and makes you feel a place'

Pilar Quintana, author of *The Bitch*

'Andrea Abreu's characters, like her sentences, are bold and wild. Reminiscent of Marieke Lucas Rijneveld's *The Discomfort of Evening*, Abreu's writing twirls and clacks with tactile precision, like winding a cassette tape with a No. 2 pencil. I'll return to *Dogs of Summer* whenever I crave a searing, brutal shot of life'

Gabriella Burnham, author of *It Is Wood, It Is Stone*

'I am overwhelmed. What a marvellous book, what a miracle'

Sara Mesa, author of *Among the Hedges*

'It describes the state of things without beating around the bush, giving way to the purest form of tenderness, innocence, and care . . . It intertwines the feeling of the first love with the pain that comes with growing up'

Brenda Navarro, author of *Empty Houses*

'*Dogs of Summer* weaves a powerful narrative, where bodies and hunger take over the story. It transports us to the threshold of puberty, to face a disturbing procession of fears, euphoria and daily violence. An unsweetened and unprejudiced portrait of poverty. Pure life'

Irene Vallejo, author of *Papyrus*

DOGS OF SUMMER

Andrea Abreu

translated by Julia Sanches

WEIDENFELD & NICOLSON

First published in Great Britain in 2022 by Weidenfeld & Nicolson
an imprint of The Orion Publishing Group Ltd
Carmelite House, 50 Victoria Embankment
London EC4Y 0DZ
An Hachette UK Company

First published in Spain as *Panza de burro* by Editorial Barrett in 2020

1 3 5 7 9 10 8 6 4 2

A CIP catalogue record for this book is
available from the British Library.

ISBN (Hardback) 978 1 4746 2406 0
ISBN (Export Trade Paperback) 978 1 4746 2407 7
ISBN (eBook) 978 1 4746 2409 1
ISBN (Audio) 978 1 4746 2410 7

Typeset by Input Data Services Ltd, Somerset
Printed and bound in Great Britain by Clays Ltd, Elcograf S.p.A.

www.weidenfeldandnicolson.co.uk
www.orionbooks.co.uk

For Lucía Díaz López, the sister I always wanted

Pure Guts and Grit

Like a cat. Isora threw up like a cat. Huckahucka-hucka and her sick splashed into the toilet bowl, then seeped into the sprawling layers of soil beneath the island. She did it two, three, four times a week. She'd say it hurts like crazy and then take her pudgy brown finger with its jaggedy, chewed-up nail and point it right at her middle, right at her belly, then throw up as casually as other people brush their teeth. She'd flush, lower the lid and with the sleeve of her sweater, which was usually white with a print of watermelon slices dotted with little black seeds, she'd wipe her mouth and carry on. She always carried on.

She never used to do it in front of me. I remember the first time I saw her throw up. It was our end-of-year party and there was lots to eat. That morning we'd set out the food on the classroom desks, which were all pushed together and covered in paper tablecloth for birthday parties. There were Munchitos potato chips, cheese doodles and Gusanitos cheese puffs. There were Conguitos chocolate sweets, Cubanitos wafers and sarnies. There were lemon donuts and tiny meringues, orange Fanta, strawberry pop, 7-Up, apple juice and pineapple juice. The two of us played at being drunk and stumbled all over the classroom with our arms around each other's shoulders, like a pair of men who had cheated on their wives and were now sick with regret.

The party ended and we headed to the canteen, where there was even more food. The cooks served us up boiled taters and ribs with corn on the cob and mojo, Isora's favourite. And when we went through with our metal trays and our rolls of bread, with our cutlery, glasses of still water (we were pretty sure it was from the tap even though you weren't meant to drink tap water on the island) and cups of Celgán yogurt, the canteen ladies asked what'll it be, red mojo or green, and Isora said red, and I thought wow, red mojo, she's such a badass, she isn't afraid of spice and she isn't afraid of grown-up food. I want to be just like her, pure guts and grit.

We sat at the table and started eating as fast as the boys racing makeshift bum boards down the road during the Tablas de San Andrés festival. Except there was nothing at the bottom to cushion our fall. Mojo dribbled down our chins, our braids were greasy from swinging into our plates and our teeth were crammed full with bits of corn and oregano – or dove cack, as Isora called the food that got stuck in the gaps. As we scoffed it all down I could already feel a sadness stampeding towards me, a stabbing pain at the pit of my stomach – and my mouth went dry, like when you eat powdered milk mixed with gofio and sugar. We wouldn't get to leave the neighbourhood that summer, and the beach was far, far away. And, unlike the girls that lived in the centre of town, we lived up in the foothills.

Isora got up from her chair and said, c'mon, Shit, I need a piss.

I got up and followed her.

I'd have followed her to the toilet or to the mouth of a vulcano. I'd have peered over the edge until I saw the dormant fire, until I felt the vulcano's dormant fire inside me.

And I followed her, though not to the canteen toilet. Instead we went to the toilet on the first floor, the one that was empty all the time and that people said was haunted by the ghost of a little girl who'd eat your turd if you cheated on your homework.

I peed, then took a step back so that Isora could go. After Isora went, after she pulled up her trousers and I saw her hairy minky like a fern fanned out on the mountain soil, she hugged the white toilet bowl, held out her middle and index fingers and shoved them down her throat. I'd never seen anything like it. Though I can't say I saw it that time either. I turned to face the mirror. I heard her cough like a small, starved animal and saw the eyes in my reflection go wide like two fists. Panic clouded my face, fear pinched the underside of my skin, Isora's throat burned – and I just stood there and did nothing.

I heard her throw up.

I pictured the Virgen de Candelaria medallion dangling from her neck, dangling over the water that would carry away everything she'd hurled into it.

Jus a Teeny Bit

Doña Carmen, d'you ever make Maggi soup, the instant kind? Isora asked the old lady. No, miniña. Why? My nan says Maggi's for skanks. Ah miniña, I don't know about that. I make soup with the hens I raise. Doña Carmen had a screw loose but a good heart. Lots of folks looked down on her because, as Nana said, she was touched. Doña Carmen was always forgetting things. She'd walk around for hours on end, reciting prayers only she knew. She had a dog with bottom teeth that stuck out the way they do on camels. Git, you lousy old mutt. Clear off or you'll have the devil to pay, she said. Sometimes she put her hand on his head, all gentle like. Other times she yelled scat, beat it, you hellhound. Doña Carmen never remembered much, but she was generous. She liked it when Isora came to visit. She lived below the church in a small white stone house with a green door and old roof tiles covered in mildew and lizards and the soles of sneakers that'd been brought over from Caracas, Venezuela, and with verode bushes that were so big they may as well have been trees. Doña Carmen never remembered much, except to peel taters. Now that was one thing she could do. She peeled them in circles. She stood them up and, with a wood-handled knife, shucked off the skin in a single long necklace. Doña Carmen liked to have eggs and fries for her afternoon snack. Isora'd bring her eggs and taters from her nan's market, and Doña Carmen would set some aside for her to snack on. She always let me have some too if I was with her. Even though she fed me taters, I knew Doña Carmen didn't like me nearly as much as she liked Isora. Isora was good at talking to old people. I just stood there and listened. How's about some coffee, misniñas? I'm not allowed to drink coffee, I said. I'll have a teeny bit, said Isora. Jus a teeny bit. It was always jus a teeny bit with Isora. She'd try anything. One time she ate some pet food they sold at the minimarket because she wanted to see how it made her feel. She'd try anything and then, if she didn't like it, she'd puke it up. I was scared my parents would smell the coffee on my breath and ground me, but Isora wasn't scared of anything. Even when her nan threatened to smack her senseless she wasn't scared. She thought you only live once, so you'd better try a teeny bit of everything when you got the chance. How's about a teeny bit of anis, miniña? Jus a teeny bit. Jus a teeny bit, she said.

Isora drank the splash of coffee left in Doña Carmen's mug, then held out her hand right away and took the small glass of Anís del Mono that the old lady had poured for her. Isora burped, she burped like five times in a row. Then Isora yawned. That's when Doña Carmen took hold of her chin and looked deep into her green eyes, into her eyes green like green grapes. She rooted around Isora's eyes like she was mining for groundwater in the mountains. The old woman shrank back. Is somebody jealous of you, miniña? Isora froze. Why, Doña Carmen? What's wrong? Miniña, you've got th'evil eye. For the love of God, head over to Eufrasia's and get yourself blessed. Tell your nan to take you to church to get prayed for too, she knows bout these sortsa things.

The five o'clock telenovela was playing as we walked out the door. At that time of day, a huge blanket of clouds usually settled over the rooftops of the houses in the neighbourhood. They weren't showing *Pasión de Gavilanes* any more. Instead, it was *La mujer en el espejo*. The lead was the same woman who played Jimena in *Pasión*, but me and Isora didn't like it as much. It was June and the neighbourhood hadn't been decked out yet with little papers for the fiesta and it'd be a long time before that happened. From Doña

Carmen's front window you could see the ocean and the sky. The ocean and the sky, which always looked like one great big thing, the same dense, grey mass as ever. It was June, but it could've been any other month of the year, in any other part of the world. It could've been a hilly town in the north of England, a place where the sky was never clear and never blue-blue, a place where the sun was more like a distant memory. It was June and classes had only ended a day ago, but I was already dead-tired and sad like low clouds hung over my head. It didn't feel like summer. Dad worked in construction and Ma worked cleaning hotels. They both worked in the South, but sometimes Ma also cleaned a couple of the neighbourhood's holiday homes, which were right around the corner from our house, up Donkey's Pass. They went South early and came home late, leaving me and Isora trapped in the jumble of houses, pine trees and steep roads at the very tip-top of town. It was June and I was sad. It was June and now I was scared too.

When we walked out of Doña Carmen's door, a worm squirmed around in my throat. The worm was black, and it told me that there were times when I got jealous of Isora. I liked the colour of her arms and her hair. I liked her handwriting. She wrote the letter *g* with a huge tail that muddled the words on the line below. I liked her eyes and a bunch of other things too. I was jealous of how she talked to grown-ups. She could barge into a conversation and say no, you're thinking of the Gloria that lives round the bend, Moreiva's ma is a different Gloria. I was jealous because her boobs were soft and round like sugar-coated gummy bears, even though she hated them. Because she got her period and had pubes on her minky, a bajillion black pubes that were coarse and pointy like the fake grass around the holiday homes. I was jealous of the Gameboi cartridge that her second cousin, who worked in IT and lived in Santa Cruz, had pirated for her. I was jealous because she had Hamtaro on her cartridge and I loved that game.

Isora didn't have a mother. She lived with her Tía Chuchi and her nan Chela, who ran the neighbour-hood minimarket. The fact that she didn't have a mother didn't make me jealous, honest. The fact that she didn't have a mother and that her aunt and nan looked after her didn't make me jealous, honest. The honest truth was that I was scared someone would tell her it was me who gave her the evil eye. Chela, Isora's nan, believed in those kinds of things. And if she found out I had done that to her granddaughter, she'd crack me on the head. Isora's nan was a fat lady with a moustache. She was a fat lady with a mous-tache who was always spoiling for a fight. Her name was Graciela, but everybody called her Chela the

Shopkeeper. She was super-religious and had a huge potty mouth too. Because she was super-religious, her other nickname was Chela the Saint. She spent every second of her spare time – and there wasn't much of it – praying and talking to the pastor and zhuzhing up the church with calla lilies and ferns that she picked from the side of her house, as well as bushels of echium, whose flowers were like white fluff that fell from the sky. Another thing Isora's nan loved to do was tell us girls everything there was to know about being fat. Or about being skinny, really. If you want to be skinny, you've got to eat on a smaller plate, she'd say, and if you want to be skinny, you've got to eat less fried taters, and one fried tater counts for two stewed taters, and what those little skanks need to do is stop eating so much candy, and I should give the girl a paddling so that she quits eating garbage, and I've got my girl on a diet 'cause she's packing it on, and if I give her an inch she takes a mile, she eats gummy bears and gets beastly fat, she eatsandeats and gets the shits and then spends three days on the toilet like a hoopoe, she eatsandeats and I can hear her retching, she spews out her guts and gets the shits and then she eats and shits and spews and pops Fortasec like it's candy, and she eats and shits and shits and shits and spews, and when she gets so blocked up that you can't even fit a piece of straw up her butthole she sticks in a couple of suppositories so she can take another shit. And she'll make herself sick. She's the devil's spawn, that girl, and she'll make herself sick from eating too much.

Isora hated her nan with a passion. At school she learned that bitch meant puta, and from that day on, whenever her nan told her go take Doña Carmen some taters and eggs, go ring up that woman, go grab the girl two cases of chicken thighs, and four rolls of bread and two hundred grams of Merican cheese and two hundred and fifty grams of goat's cheese, and go get that girl a hunk of guava paste, plus a sack of taters, and go fetch her some prawns, and go ring up that forener, seeing as you speak English and the only language I know is Christian, Isora would say, all right, bitch, I'm going bitch, I got it bitch, whatever you want bitch, thank you bitch, will you be needing anything else bitch? And her nan would eye her distrustingly and Isora would explain that bitch meant grandmother in English.

The other person who worked at the minimarket was Chuchi. Chuchi was Isora's aunt and Chela's second daughter. Everyone called Chuchi Chuchi, but nobody knew her real name. Chuchi had green eyes like Isora but with brown smudges that spilled into the whites. Like coffee dregs at the bottom of a mug. Chuchi was tall and skinny with long legs, hollow cheeks and raisiny skin. Apart from her eyes, she looked nothing like Isora. Chuchi'd never been seen with a boyfriend and she didn't have kids. She was big on church too. Unlike her mother, who dreamed of becoming a saint, Chuchi's dream was to be a saleswoman. For a while she sold make-up and face cream and hair soap and body soap all over the neighbourhood. She went around in her secretary clothes, with a suit jacket that was green like her eyes and a skirt that was green like Isora's green eyes and brown block-heel boots, with a binder full of Avon catalogues of products that she showed off to all of the women, from house to house. Chela was always saying that her daughter was going to rack and ruin from walking the streets all day like a tramp.

We walked up the road until we reached the front of the minimarket. Isora didn't stop to talk to her nan. Where d'you think you're going? Isn't there room for you at home? Chela yelled at us from the counter, crowded with people. All you two ever do is go round sticking your noses where they don't belong! Isora carried on walking uphill like it was nothing. I followed her and glanced over at Chuchi and at Chela. Chuchi was slicing cold meats, her head hung low as she listened to Chela chiding us, and it was as if she had a weight on the nape of her neck, as if she was carrying her mother like a kestrel perched on the tiptop of her spine. Let's go to Eufrasia's and have her bless me before the old bitch finds out, Isora said. And the black worm squirmed back. I didn't know much about evil eye. I knew that when lil babies were pink and bald and ugly and had no teeth and their heads were covered in scabs, people tied small red ribbons to their prams because their mothers and grandmas were scared. Scared, my nana said, of th' evil eye. If people stared at the lil babies for too long or whispered nice things to them, like what a sweet angel, God bless him, God bless his little soul, how old is he, he's so handsome, their mothers and grandmas would tense up like a dead man's leg. Whenever Nana saw a newborn, the first thing she did was cross herself and say God bless him from the tips of his toes to his belly button. From the tips of the toes to his belly button and nothing above that, I thought. Which is why I was convinced I could only get evil eye around my minky and my butt and my leg hair, which I had begged Ma to shave for me even though she always refused flat out. Isora and me did a bunch of things with our bodies, from the tips of our toes to our belly buttons. And specially around our minkies. So maybe evil eye had to do with that. But I kept quiet about it, I kept quiet and we kept walking.

Isora Candelaria González Herrera

When we got to Eufrasia's, Isora stood at the door and looked at me and said you knock, and I knocked, then took a step back, and out came Eufrasia in a kitchen apron splattered with blood. Miniña, Carmitas called. C'min, I was jus carvin' some rabbit for dinner. Sit, sit. Ay, miniña, go'on and have a seat, she said to Isora, and then sat her down on a plastic lawn chair in the middle of a jungle of ferns that were big and green like the ones up on Monte del Agua. While Isora settled in, I pulled up a chair and sat in a corner because I wasn't famous. Isora was the one with evil eye, she was the one who got those sorts of things, nothing ever happened to me. My nana was always saying that I had a knotty gut, but no one ever took *me* to get blessed.

Eufrasia crossed herself and, since I didn't know what to do, I crossed myself too, but in a real quiet way, like when you wave hello to someone who doesn't wave back, then scratch your cheek to cover it up. She turned to Isora and crossed herself and then started saying on the cross He suffered and on the cross He died and Christ on the cross I bless you, and Isora looked at Eufrasia and Eufrasia's eyes were big and wide like wreckfish eyes, and the woman moved her mouth and rubbed her fingers, which were wrinkled like the dried bark on a grapevine, gnarled and chapped from years of bleach and dirt. And my Lord Jesus Christ, the world you did wander, and many were the miracles you worked, and many the poor you healed, and Mary Magdalene did you forgive, and the holy tree of the cross, and the woman's eyes went white, paler-than-a-notecard white, and she rubbed her hands together faster and faster, and harder and harder, and I looked at Isora and her face was calm but focused, she had the Virgen de Candelaria medallion in her mouth and she looked happy because she was being healed. And I kept thinking she's gonna die, she's gonna die, Lucifer's gonna shoot out of Eufrasia's eyes and kill her. And Saint Anne birthed Mary, and Saint Isabel birthed John the Baptist, and they baptized Him in the River Jordan, and John asked the Lord: I, Lord who have been blessed by your hallowed hands, and Eufrasia rubbed her hands together and her legs shuddered and her eyes twitched like when dogs chase cats in their dreams, and just as these words, her eyes teared up and skittered around their sockets, are right, and her hair stood on end, and true, and she started swallowing hard, may you clear away the fire, the air, and she burped, the evil air, and burped, the evil eye, and burped, from her stomach and her head, and burped, and spat, from her joints and her back, may you clear it all away and send it to the bottom of the ocean, and she sprayed spit in the air and it slabbered me in the face, where neither I nor any other creature can be harmed by it, and she threw up some of her afternoon soup and then frothed at the mouth, she frothed at the mouth like when dogs have rabies, as Nana said, she frothed like those dogs that get put down for biting someone, and as Isora watched her she chewed on her gold chain, she was always getting a sore throat from so much suckinsuckin on the chain that her mother had given her when she was just born and that her nan had had adjusted for her in town more than a hundred times, because Isora's neck kept growing bigger and bigger while the chain got smaller and smaller and her nan said she'd choke to death if she kept it that short, but Isora liked wearing the chain skin-tight because she said it was sexier that way. The Virgen de Candelaria was Isora's favourite saint, which is why she wore her medallion on a chain around her neck. Like when people have a favourite

Pokémon or a favourite Bratz doll and wear a tiny Charmander around their neck, except the chain was much more important to her than Pokémon was to me because she'd got the medallion from her mother, who she loved to bits because she hadn't known her very long, her mother, who she adored to bits because she'd never had the chance to crack Isora on the head like her nan was always doing. Most of all because she and the Virgen Morenita had the same name because Isora was called Isora Candelaria, Isora Candelaria González Herrera.

Then Isora said she's choking, Eufrasia's choking! And the woman looked up and her mouth was all slimy like a slug that's been crawling all over the patio, and her face looked like it was made of slimy slug trails, and she said and if this is not enough, may the grace of God be enough, God is great.

Amen!

Praised be!

And Eufrasia prayed the Creed. And I prayed too. But no one had taught me how, and I was a bag of nerves, so I just moved my mouth like psspsspsspss until Isora said that's me healed, chacha. Let's get back to the minimarket.

We stepped outside and saw Gaspacho licking his willy. The moment he spotted us he started barking, aroorooroo, and it sounded like when you try and talk underwater. We set off and the dog followed us at least halfway back, to Melva's place, right by the great big pond where my ma and uncle and Isora's mother and aunt had all learned to swim, and my ma told me that Grandpa used to toss her in with a rope tied round her waist and that you learned to swim because you had to, which is the best way to learn things, but Grandpa had gone away to live with another woman so people never talked about him any more, or about the pond, or about being taught to swim, which was why we never learned. And the dog kept following us and we said go'on up, Gaspa, ssssht, and Eulalia came out of her house and said giiiiiiiit Gaspachocabrón, get your sorry butt home now! And the dog went and sat in the middle of the road, and that's where he stayed as we carried on downhill.

Like Desert Truffles
Under Pine Needles

Navy-blue, pink, yellow, more yellow, burnt yellow, fried-yolk yellow and red. That's what the houses in the neighbourhood were like, bright and colourful, like the squares on a Ludo board. They came in all kinds of colours and were either half-started or half-done. At any rate, none of the houses were finished, they were all imperfect monsters. Nearly every house had at least one bit left without whitewash, the exposed cinder blocks stained with mildew and rising damp. Nearly every house had been built by the people who lived in them. Stone by stone, block by block. Nearly every house had been built without a permit. Nearly every house belonged to a single family: the Smokes family, the Tussler family, the Pickers, the Mourners, the Horse family, our Chinese friends, the Scrubs, our Black friends. Like birds that set up their nests right next to each other, one on top of the other, to keep safe.

And all at a slant. A vertical neighbourhood on a vertical mountain crowded with low-bellied clouds and sliced through by a long, wide cave-like tunnel that went from the tip-top of the mountain all the way to the ocean, like the mantle in the song about the Virgen de Candelaria, the prettiest saint, the one with the darkest skin. So vertical that sometimes it seemed like the shiny bee-em-dub-yous would skid all the way down, music blasting. That they'd grow wings and fly us to San Marcos beach. But that didn't happen, it never happened. Instead the drivers would set their handybrakes and shift into first gear, then cross themselves as they burned rubber uphill. They always crossed themselves when they passed the church of the Virgen del Rosario.

There were two kinds of houses in our neighbourhood, and they were all jumbled together. Some were old, like Doña Carmen's and my nana's. Those ones were stone and had small inner patios with bedrooms laid around them. Patios with roofs made of wriggly tin that my nana called wiggly tin and that people had started saying gave you cancer. A patio that let in a light so bright, a light stored for so many thousands of years, that it set all the canaries aflutter in their cages and had them singing out of control – peepeepeepeepeepee – from the first glow of day until nightfall. And the ferns and the bougainvillea that crept through the gap between the front door and the wiggly tin roof were out of control too. When the light hit them, the plants shot up so fast it was like they were walking up the walls, like they were dancing on the walls.

Then there were the other, more modern houses. The ones that belonged to the younger people who worked in the South in construction and cleaning hotels, the ones with the shiny bee-em-dub-yous in metallic blue, metallic red and metallic yellow with carriages that hugged the ground, so low that when they drove up through the neighbourhood they left half their car bits behind them, and played 'Pobre diabla' at full blast and 'Agüita' and 'Mentirosa' and 'Una ráfaga de amor' at full blast and 'Felina' a gazillion times at full blast. Those ones, the new houses, were two storeys tall and had a load of windows and banisters and a gate, most of all they had a gate, a real big one, a huge one, an enormous one that could let in a truck the size of a pine tree, all fuzzy with pine needles, filled with bananas and tomatoes and presents like Babybjörns and Barbies dressed up as nurses. Those were the most colourful of all the houses – they were pink, yellow, even yellower and fried-yolk yellow. Venezuelan-style, they said. Like the houses in Venezuela, *dafuck*.

The topmost houses grew up from the ground like desert truffles under pine needles when the rain got the earth damp. The first houses in the neighbourhood grew up from the earth next to a skirt of pine trees at the foothills of the vulcano – vulcano my nana called it, and she always said skirt like the vulcano was Shakira. There were pine cones all over the roof tiles and roof terraces of the topmost houses in the neighbourhood, and a lot of the time they looked less like houses built by humans than places where witches and elves might live. As for the rest of the neighbourhood, everything but the houses was dark green, the colour of the forest. On clear days you could see the vulcano. It almost never happened, but everyone knew that behind the clouds lived a giant who was 3,718 metres tall and could set fire to all of us if he wanted.

My house was a mountain of houses built on top of my great-grandma Edita's house, the only one with a permit, the only one that had a number on it. Since my house was made up of a bunch of other houses, we had to coordinate whenever we wanted to watch TV or cook food. If we turned on two ovens at the same time, the power blew. If Ma and Dad and Nana and Nana's brother Tío Ovidio and me, meaning everyone who lived in that house, turned on every TV at the same time, I'd feel like the house was exploding and I was flying up, up in the air.

Below our house was Juanita Banana's and below his the Cueva del Viento, and further down from the cave

lived a German woman who'd give me skipping ropes
as presents, and below her you had the house of a man
called Gracián whose eyebrows were like two centipedes sticky-taped to his face, and below him lived
this girl called Saray, who was two years older and sort
of our friend except she acted like she was this big-
deal celebrity because her parents ran a bar, and below
her house you had Eulalia's place, where the women
in the neighbourhood got together to peel taters and
yak about the fact that Antonio's girl Zuleyma was
getting kind of chunky, and about what'd happened
the day before on *El diario de Patricia*, and below that
lived a girl who went to university in La Laguna and
when she came home at weekends said things like my
friends yea beer yea my cousin yea panties yea, and my
ma would turn round and ask me if uni made people
stupid. And below that you had Eufrasia's house, and
below her lived a cousin of Nana's whose house was
surrounded by grapevines and orange trees and who
people said kept two women under his roof, his wife
and her sister, who was like their servant, because
his sister-in-law took care of the property while his
wife just sat around all dollied up, and below that
you had Melva's house, and then the gayhouse, and
then Conchi's house, and right below Conchi's was
Isora's minimarket, and opposite the minimarket
was the cultural centre, and below the cultural centre

was the bar, and below the bar was Doña Carmen's house, and beyond that I had no idea, because as far as I was concerned Doña Carmen's house was the end of the world.

Looks Like Rain

On the Night of San Juan, Nana built a gigantic fire. She built it in the middle of the garden, and it was several metres tall. On the Night of San Juan, you couldn't breathe for all the dry grass that folks were burning after collecting it all year long. Billows of smoke joined the blanket of clouds that skulked over the neighbourhood and formed a heavy white mass that stuck to our skin. Pieces of car tyres and paper rained down from the sky. It was me, Nana, Tío Ovidio and my ma and dad. From the attic you could see the whole neighbourhood covered all over in small dots of fire. The swallows had been in a frenzy all afternoon, chittering away as Nana and Dad tossed in the debris from that year's building projects, as well as all the plants they'd weeded out. Looks like rain, Ovidio kept saying as he watched the birds darting frantically across the sky, looks like rain.

In the middle of the bonfire there was a doll with eyes painted with a felt-tip pen and a hat from Los Dos Caminos hardware store. Dad grabbed an old mop handle and dressed it in Grandpa's old clothes: a blue-and-white striped shirt that was too tight on him and had a large breast pocket – I remember how his belly used to jut out, big and round like a boulder – and a pair of black pleated trousers, also his. When I saw the clothes they'd picked out for the doll I got nervous, because what if Grandpa decided to leave the German lady one day, then came home and started asking for his clothes.

Only after the doll's body turned to pure ash did the raindrops start falling. Summer rain made me uneasy. First came the damp, then the cascade of water rushing down the road, then the puddles in the furrows. Nana had some taters baking in the fire. By the time we rushed out of the garden, the rain had put out the last flames. As I ran I had the feeling that even though Isora and me had vowed to do whatever it took to get to the beach that summer, it wasn't gonna happen. Everybody worked round the clock. Dad said he was riding the dollar, which was why he needed to go South on Sundays too. We headed back into Nana's house. There was grilled pineapple and coriander mojo. We ate the chinegua taters we'd harvested in June, when I was still in school. I hadn't helped because on the Sunday they decided to pick them, I was working on a project with Isora. I hated harvesting taters. We had to get up early and throw on old sneakers and clothes, then spend all morning bent over – Nana and me and Ma, if she wasn't away cleaning one of the holiday homes – gathering the taters that Dad and my uncles dug up. Nana and me sorted through them on the go, tossing the big taters in one bucket and the small ones in another. Daddy always said I was a lost soul, that I was a lost soul because I drove him crazier than a minister. When we did the taters, my back hurt like hell and my boogers went pitch-black like asphalt. The only thing that made me feel better was when I picked them out and rolled them between my fingers. Just me and my black snot, far away from the buckets of taters.

When we were done eating, I went to Nana's kitchen cupboard and grabbed a bar of La Candelaria chocolate. I broke off a piece with my fingers and scraped the chocolate with my teeth like a sad little mouse. I thought of Isora and wondered if she, her nan and her aunt were eating grilled pineapple too, and if she was wishing for the beach as much as me. I went into the TV room and picked up the phone. I dialled Chela's number. Sup, Shit? Isora said. I'm bored, the fire went out. Am I coming by early tomorrow? I asked her. Yeawhynot, Shit. Bring your swimsuit, in case somebody can shift us to the beach.

I got into bed early just so I could lie there and think about the beach. Last time I went because Dad wanted to fish at Punta de Teno and me and Ma had tagged along. It was Easter and blustery, but I got in anyway. My ma sat on top of a crag where she could keep an eye on me because Nana always said the ocean's the devil and the girl's no good in the water, and she ate pumpkin seeds and flipped through cross-stitch magazines and home décor magazines for rustic-style houses. The tide was high. I stayed near the edge and dunked my head all the way to the bottom, grabbed fistfuls of pebbles and tried to bring them all the way back up. But when I got to the surface, my hands were practically empty. One time, I wound up with a small, empty burgado seashell that looked like a shiny, worn moon.

Sunscream, Sunscream
Round Her Neck

We spent all morning trying to find someone to take us to San Marcos, but everybody said no. The old ladies were the only ones who wanted to come because they couldn't get enough of Isora, except they didn't have cars and they didn't know how to drive either, and it's not like they were gonna walk the three hours there and back with us and, anyhow, the pavement was super-narrow and the cars got real close. We figured we could go on our own. Isora gathered up all the stuff we'd need and shoved it in a backpack: the towel, the sunscream, the swimsuits and a couple of Revilla chorizo and cheese sarnies. Chela was at the counter and heard the clatter coming from the room beneath the minimarket, where Isora was rummaging for a pair of old sneakers. She rushed downstairs to find us. And where the hell do you think you're going? To the beach, bitch, Isora said. Chela pulled off her slipper

29

so she could hurl it at Isora's head and screamed I'll show you a beach, you little cunt! I cowered against one of the shelves that was stacked with bottles of Libby's juice covered in dust and cobwebs. Isora ran behind the fridgerators and started muttering foquin bitch, foquin bitch, I wish you'd die, you foquin bitch. Cheeeeee, muchacha, the candy guy's up here waiting for you! yelled an old woman from the market door. Chela rushed upstairs still clutching her slipper. Iso, you can come out now. Your nan's gone upstairs, I said, and peeled myself away from the shelves. I said it again and waited, but she stayed behind the fridgerators. I sat on a plastic crate in a corner of the room and waited a while longer. At one point I thought she must've fallen asleep or that maybe she was touching herself because her breathing sounded heavy, but I couldn't bring myself to check. I was kind of scared, I don't know why. About an hour or so later she crawled out from behind the fridgerators like a poisoned lizard and said, Shit, come to the bathroom with me, I'm about to crap myself. I looked at her and saw that her eyes were froggy, like she'd been crying.

We ate at Nana's. We ate fried chicken wings, stewed taters and red mojo. Nana's mojo was runny because she mixed in water from the well. Olive oil had been hard to come by when she was small, and she'd just never kicked the habit. We ate gofio

amasado too. Nana put the gofio dough in a bowl and
we each tore off a piece, rolled them into little balls
and dunked the balls in the runny mojo. She let us
eat everything with our hands because, according to
Nana, it was yummier that way. Whenever Chela saw
us eating like that she'd say we were pigs and then ask
me how my nana let us get away with that disgustful
behaviour. And when she said 'your gran' I could hear
the resentment in her voice. She knew that Nana was
too soft on us. When we were done eating, Isora said
she had an idea. We should go to the canal and pretend it was San Marcos beach.

On our way out we grabbed a couple of Tío Ovidio's
gardening hats, then went next door to invite Juanita
Banana to swim and monkey around with us on the
made-up canal beach. Juanita Banana cried whenever
we called him by his nickname. Isora called out his
real name and Juanita Banana came to the balcony
with an egg and pork-loin sandwich in his hand.
Juanito, come down, we're gonna pretend the canal is
a beach and trash-talk women with cellulite. I can't,
he said, Ma says I've gotta weed the garden. Juanita
Banana was hardly ever allowed to play because he
always needed to weed the garden or feed the animals
or mop the patio or wash the cars or hose down his
brother's moped. His dad wanted him to work. Juanita
hated studying, and his dad was always saying that

if he didn't study he'd send him to pick tomatoes in the fields, and sometimes I suspected that it was more than just a threat and that his dad really did want him to start picking tomatoes as a lilboy. I pictured him as an old man with a great big bald spot in the middle of his head, a head like a scorched field. I pictured him with a beard too, a beard peppered with white hairs here and there. I pictured him all grown up with a tomato cupped in his hands as the men around him said Juanita Banana this and Juanita Banana that, and he looked all glum as he thought back on the time when he was a lilboy who played Barbies with us and Ken dolls with us and used the Barbie doll to say: Heygirlmyname'sChaxiraxiandI'mcute.

The canal was below the minimarket and behind the cultural centre. The high-school boys – we called them the kinkis – met at the cultural centre to smoke weed. I always felt embarrassed walking past them because I had no clue how to act. Isora knew the name of every cultural centre boy, and she reeled them off like a song: yeray jairo eloy ancor iván acaymo. She said hi to all of them, and for her seeing them wasn't a big deal or anything, she was famous, she had a mini-market, and if they didn't say hi back her nan could turn round and not sell them their chorizo sand-wiches or their five o'clock Colas, which was when the boys got together after school to smoke weed and eat sarnies and chat on mésinye whenever there were computers available at the cultural centre, which had only got them a few months ago.

The cultural centre stank of weed, even from afar. The cops used to come through the neighbourhood all the time back then, because according to them lots of drugs were sold there. Juanita Banana told us one time that his brother said the men at Bar de Antonio did drugs there, and even though I didn't really know what drugs were or what they were good for, when Isora and Juanita talked about it I always said yeah, this place is crawling with drugs.

Isora knew about this section of the canal where some of the concrete slabs covering it were broken and you could see the water streaming down littered with pine needles and pine cones and rocks from the mountain. Our bodies were small enough to fit through that secret entrance. We followed the canal on the far side. The trail was super-narrow and one wrong step could mean ending up smashed to pieces like a rabbit. When we got to the section of the canal with the lifted-up slabs we could see the whole town, every last bit of it. There was Redondo, the neighbourhood to the left, and all the other neighbourhoods around ours whose names we didn't even know. All under a cover of clouds and drizzle, of dark-grey gloom. We looked out at the centre of town and at the lower neighbourhoods, at the lucky neighbourhoods all aglow in bright yellow, and behind them, right in front of the ocean, was San Marcos beach. Chos, said Isora, and her eyebrows arched so high they just about touched her hairline, 'magine being born near the beach.

We took our towels out of our backpacks and set them folded on the edge of the canal entrance. Me and Isora didn't wear our bikini tops out because Chela and my ma wouldn't let us. Besides, Isora said that girls who wore bikini tops were sluts and that they'd get knocked up before all of us, and I agreed. But the honest truth was that we couldn't wait until we were finally allowed to wear them, because that way we wouldn't feel embarrassed about our puffy nipples ever again. There was no one around that day, so we decided to put on our bikini tops for the first time. Isora had two tops that her family in Santa Cruz had given her for her birthday, and she let me borrow one.

Isora took off her sneakers and slipped her feet in the water. Then it was my turn. The stream was cold, colder than the water that ran down the drains by Nana's house first thing in the morning. As we soaked our feet, I couldn't stop staring at the ocean. Shut your eyes, Shit, and picture us at San Marcos beach, said Isora. And I pictured myself walking along the water's edge. The twigs and pine cones that flowed down the canal bumped me in the ankles and I imagined they were pebbles crashing into my body, leaving my shin bones sliced up and bruised. Isora kept her eyes closed as she started the game: chacha, that blonde lady over there that's getting in the water, d'you know who she is? Yeah, isnit María? Yeah, María, the town bike, they say she's got two boyfrens on the go at the same time. Isn't she married? I asked, screwing my eyes shut. Yeah, but Moreiva, the one round the bend, told me she's a slut and that she's always going round bars tryina pick up men and that she's a drunk. I cracked open an eye and saw Isora seated above the canal making circles with her feet in the water. She was scratching at the sides of her minky because it itched all the time from shaving. She scratched herself, and then carried on: and Doña Carmen bought her a mattress 'cause she doesn't even care if her kids sleep on the floor. I looked at her thighs covered in soft, long fuzz, like the kind on a plush toy, and dotted all over in moles. They were shiny, almost golden. Eulalia says she was caught necking a man from the beach behind Plaza San Marcos on the day of the Baile de Magos, she went on. I ran my eyes from the tips of her toes, which were pudgy with dug-in toenails trimmed down to the quick, all the way up to her minky, then closed them again. As she told me all about María the town bike I had a crystal-clear, realer-than-real image of the two of us all grown up, sunbathing on San Marcos beach, our legs and staches waxed. I was rubbing sunscream on Isora's thighs. I was stroking the tops of her thighs and she was stretched out like a cat. Her moles sucked up all the sunscream and I had to squeeze more out of the yellow bottle of SPF 30 into my right hand and then rub sunscream on her thighs again. I felt Isora's ingrown hairs beneath my fingers. I felt the hairs on her thighs again, pushing out like cannons, and again I filled every pore with sunscream and she laughed and her chin mole glowed and I rubbed her with more sunscream. Sunscream round her neck, sunscream between her fingers, sunscream on her nipples and behind her ears. Sunscream on her eyelashes, because Isora's lashes were long like worms. Her lashes were long and thin and blonde and almost see-through in the sun.

We wandered home from the canal. Isora took off her sneakers because her toenails hurt. She said chos, Shit, I shouldna trimmed them so short, and then stepped carefully on the tarmac so that she wouldn't get stabbed by the gravel, so that she wouldn't cut herself on shards of the drunks' smashed bottles. We picked loquats and nibbled on them as we made our way back down. They were hot, but Isora said it was better that way, because then they'd give her the shits and flush the food she didn't need out of her system.

I licked the gooey, dribbly loquat juice off one hand and held Isora with the other. I wished I could've held her hand the whole walk home, but all I could reach was her arm. I told myself that we weren't touchy-feely friends. The hand that held Isora's arm burned. We kept on and by the time we reached the cultural centre I had let go. The boys were done smoking weed and the streets were empty. It was dark out and the sky was a cavern. Isora went behind a line of parked cars, the ones that belonged to the men guzzling wine at Bar de Antonio, and I followed. When I caught up with her she grabbed hold of my arm, hard, like she was trying to keep from falling down a gully. I saw our bodies joined together in the rear-view mirror of a white car, the palm of her hand flush against the skin of my arm. It lasted less than a second. By the time Chela showed up at the counter, Isora had already let go.

A Metallic Bimmer Zoomed Past

At the minimarket, Chela screamed so loud that it put the fear of God in you. Those fuckers took a dump outside the market again, she said. They're at it again, the little whores. Chela claimed that when the spirit moved them the forest witches would go on such a shitspree they might as well have been hoopoes for all the gunk they left behind. She talked about the forest witches like she'd known them her whole life. The old ladies in the neighbourhood said that when they used to collect pine needles up in the forest, they'd find the witches dancing long-haired and naked, grinding against the pines. The second she saw me that day Isora said, Shit, I've gotta shovel up this witch cack. Gimme a hand, yeah? Y'know I always help you when you need it. Then we can play with our Barbies. Before I even had a chance to say yes, Isora shoved a grocery bag at me so I could deal with the humongous turd heap at the back door. Even Sinson's chewed-up quilt bed was covered in poop. Sinson was Chela's dog. His name was Sinson, like Homer from *The Sinsons*, and he was missing an eye because one day a metallic bimmer had zoomed past him in the neighbourhood and run him right over, and when he got home his eye was hanging out of its socket and Chela screamed Sweet Mother of Jesus they've ruined my puppy. And she said puppy like she had nothing but love for dogs, though if there was one thing the old ladies in our neighbourhood had in common it was that none of them could stand dogs. They thought they were foul and treated them the way they'd have liked to treat their husbands, who hung around Bar de Antonio's all the time drinking wine and playing cards.

I started cleaning because I knew Isora wouldn't lift a finger. I grabbed a hose from Chela's patio, squidged out some fairi liquid and then had at it. La bitch says it was the witches, but I bet it was that slut Saray, she said as I hosed down the rug and Sinson barked at me for touching his things. Saray who was two years older than us and lived next door to me. We played with her now and then, but Isora said she was stupid and a bit stuck-up, and she didn't really like her. Isora rolled up the hose and I dried my hands on my shirt. It got late as we chatted and washed the crap off the street. Once we had all the turds in white grocery bags, we went looking for some thick brambles to toss them in. It was almost pitch-dark. We could smell the lady of the night flower, who told us it was getting late and we should be on our way home. Right at that moment, small cracks formed in the blanket of clouds and the last light of day spilled through them, turning everything a bright golden colour. My chest felt awful tight, like I couldn't breathe. I never knew how to say goodbye to Isora. I stared at her like someone who was about to say goodbye for years.

But Isora walked me home. She always walked me home.

Then I walked her home.

Then she walked me home.

Jus like a pack of yogurts from the minimarket, she said to me once. She said it about the two of us, convinced I'd not heard her even though I had. Just like those packs of yogurts that always come in pairs.

Always, after playing with our Barbie dolls all day long and pretending they were characters in a tele-novela, that the Ken dolls were Juan, Franco and Gato and the Barbie dolls were Jimena, Sarita and Norma, that the Ken dolls were big, tan brutes and the Barbie dolls were skinny, real skinny, super-skinny and that they were good dancers and good kissers too, and that they jumped on the Ken dolls and the Ken dolls jumped on them, and we shoved their small plastic bodies together, wickiwickiwicki, and said they were loving each other the way Jimena loved Óscar and Norma loved Juan and Franco loved Sarita and Franco loved Rosario and Franco loved Rosario and Franco loved Rosario, and Rosario was the biggest slut of them all but she was also the best dancer, and that's why we always fought over who got to be Rosario or Jimena or, last of all, Norma, but never Sarita because we thought Sarita was the boringest and the thickest, Sarita was like Cactus in *The Power-puff Girls* and she made us sick. Always, after playing with our Barbie dolls and pretending Juan had argued with the other dolls and thumped Franco for hooking up with Rosario and then thumped Nana's cats and then thumped the mouldy walls in the back of Nana's house and then thumped the air with thumpy thumps and love-sick thumps, Isora would walk me home, she always walked me home. She'd come to the front door with me, and the roosters and the birds and even the rabbits who can't make any sounds (except maybe wakawakawakawaka) would cry because they heard us at the door. Then Isora would step away and say see ya tomorrow, Shit. She called me Shit in an affection-ate way and it was a small, shy, quiet affection. See ya tomorrow, Shit, see ya tomorrow, and then she'd head up the hill with her high ponytail swinging side to side like a pendulum, left-right, left-right, left-right,

right-left, and when she was halfway gone and nearly out of sight, when all I could see was her hair swinging without a body beneath it, she'd turn around and yell c'mon, walk me back, chacho, y'know I always walk you. And then the two of us would retrace the whole of our zigzaggedy steps, left-right, left-right, left-right, right-left, because Isora said you got less tired if you walked that way, and we started talking about the time we'd peed ourselves just to see what it felt like, we'd done it in a tater field that belonged to one of Nana's neighbours who grew loads of different things, and then we'd rolled around on the ground covered in piss, and before we knew it we were at the gayhouse and it wouldn't be long until we reached the minimarket, which is when Isora asked me if I remembered the time in school when we poured apple juice on the head of this girl we didn't like and got detention. The golden light had stopped spilling through the gaps in the clouds, I looked up at the sky and it was almost night. I asked Isora if she remembered that time in school when we'd played at dogs and how Josito, Redondo's kid, had been her dog and had waggled around on all fours with a rope tied to his neck, and if you asked he'd give you his paw and also stick up his leg to pretend-pee on the school walls, which were painted with pictures of the Canary Islands and of itty-bitty people dressed as wizards and with lady

wizards and bunches of bananas and bullock carts and
with taters and mortar guns from when we celebrated
the Day of the Canary Islands, and then Isora yelled
shut your hole you puto mutt, shush you puto foquin
mutt, and I laughed and laughed because I loved it
when Isora said puto, my ears filled with honey when
Isora said

puto
puto foquin mutt
puto foul mutt stank
puto Sinson you son of a foquin puta
puto skank
puto birdbrain
shifty puto
puto retard
puto crapheap
bitch foquin puta
more puta than a puto chicken

Before we realized, we were at Melva's. Isora's nan
called her the Shack because, even though she wasn't
married, she was shacked up with some Scottish guy.
We were just around the corner from the minimarket.
We carried on walking and thinking of the time when
we'd gone to Mass and sat in the front pew and Isora'd
started imitating the pastor and I'd burst out laughing,
I'd laughed so hard that the pastor had to stop and tell
me to stand at the church door, and all the old ladies

in the neighbourhood had given me dirty looks, and as we thought back on it I remembered that when I'd stood there on my own with all the old ladies looking at me I got this scared feeling because I knew they hadn't liked me before, that they'd liked Isora better, and I was sure they'd like me even less now, but I kept it all to myself.

And we carried on walking.

And we made it to the minimarket.

And we did it all over again.

See ya tomorrow, Shit, she said. See ya tomorrow. I walked up the road and when I was halfway home I got sad and stared up at the sky, and it was properly night now and the frogs in the pond that nobody swam in any more started ribbiting, and the sound they made was like a song. A centuries-old song from back when Isora and me weren't friends yet, even though it was our destiny, because if there was one thing I knew it was that me and Isora were made the way things that are born to live and die together are made, and I turned round and I said walk me back, at least as far as the gayhouse, walk me back, c'mon, y'know I always walk you.

The Tourists Were Disgusting Slobs

I both liked and didn't like the holiday homes. What I mean is: I liked them because they were pretty, but I didn't like them because between us there was a barrier of clear clingfilm, of plastic wrap that stopped me from enjoying the best things about the holiday homes. The holiday homes were on the next street over from ours, up Donkey's Pass. The holiday homes were to blame for the fact that on the days Ma didn't have to go and clean hotels in the South she still had to clean the holiday homes, and that meant we couldn't go to the beach, which is the main reason I didn't like the holiday homes. If I wanted to spend time with Ma I had to clean the holiday homes with her, but cleaning holiday homes was the boringest thing in the world. Sometimes she told me to sit and play nice and quiet but when I played nice and quiet an emptiness grew in my belly and made me feel blue. At the same time, when she didn't let me play and instead asked me to help with the cleaning, that didn't make me happy either, because I hated cleaning holiday homes.

When I grew up I wanted to be an office secretary, not a house cleaner.

There was a special area of the holiday homes that we could go into and the clients couldn't. That's what Ma called the foreners. Clients. The area we could go into stank of damp and was full of cobwebs and dirt stains on the white walls, which had turned the colour of cinnamon. Ma and the gardener called it the tool room. I felt special when I was in the tool room. Except then I realized that the foreners were even specialer because they could lie on their sun loungers and read their huge books (I didn't enjoy reading at all, much as I wanted to) and wash in the outdoor shower and eat at the tables beneath the parasols, which I called umbrellas and were made of dried palm leaves, and sleep in beds with white sheets under mosquito nets strung over their heads like they were in the jungle.

My ma ran the dishwasher with bleach to get out all the gunk the tourists left on the dishes, because tourists were disgusting slobs who didn't know how to clean up after themselves, and did they not clean their own houses or what. Ma said that if I thought that was gross, I should see what they did in the hotels, and then she wondered aloud if they behaved that

way at home too. In the hotel rooms they left crap on
the outside of the toilet bowl and took dumps in the
waste baskets, like dogs, like gross stinking dogs. Ma
would hold her breath as she cleaned, then spend the
rest of the day on edge. Ma wiped the dried bits of
egg and the yolky egg stains off the dishes, forks and
glasses, which were also stained from people eating
and drinking with their eggy hands, and then sent
me to sweep the leaves and the rotted figs splattered
on the patio around the pool. That's where I saw the
tourists doing touristy things while I swept. In those
moments, I would picture I was a client with client
children who wore one-piece swimsuits, even though
I didn't understand why anyone'd wear a one-piece
swimsuit, and that I went swimming in the pool.
Daydreaming, I'd leave the broom and the shovel
against the wall and creep up to the edge. I'd stand
in front of the clients with my hands behind my back.
The kids that were playing would stop and stare at
me like they'd seen a ghost, then try and figure out
why there was a girl cleaning the patio like she was
a house cleaner. And for a second I'd feel powerful,
but then the kids would jump in the pool and start
splashing about, and as the heat pressed down on my
head a thin layer of clingfilm would show up in front
of my eyes and I'd realize that I wasn't a client, I was
the cleaning lady's daughter – cleaning lady is what

they called her – and if I didn't finish sweeping up the leaves she'd get cross with me. So I'd gather up all the little leaves and think about how I wasn't a client and I wasn't any good at house-cleaning either. Whenever Nana saw Ma cleaning she'd tell her that she was like an axe, chop-chop. That she was like a flash of lightning. Whenever I heard her say that I'd think about how I'd never be even half as fast as she was. And then my ma would come out and tell me to get a move on, muchachita, quit standing around like a lost soul, and all of a sudden my arms and legs would freeze up and some force would stop me from sweeping and make me stand there, my eyes fixed on the clients and a dumb look on my face. And the more Ma said to get a move on, you little devil, snap out of it, the slower I worked. Which is why sometimes she told me to sit and play nice and quiet. Because I slowed Ma down as I stared through the barrier of clingfilm between me and the clients.

Rabbit in a Single Bite

La bitch has me on a diet again, Isora said on the phone. An onion diet. She's making me eat onion soup every meal for two weeks. Ew, that's gross, I said. Come over, Shit, I'm dying to bake something but I can't eat it, all I can eat is this dumb soup. Come over, Shit, so I can watch you eat cake. Gimme a sec, I said.

Out on the street there was the rumble of cement mixers. There was always something that needed building in the neighbourhood, and every day you could hear the sound of cement mixers churning like ghosts dragging their chains on the other side of the walls. The sun wasn't out again, though you could tell it was hiding behind the clouds. The sky was like a big white wall with a yellow sun crayoned in the middle and painted over with an extra layer of white. It was boiling out. It was the haze, or calima as my dad called it. It hurt our chests to breathe and everything felt heavier than usual, like our sneakers were filled with concrete. Isora's house smelled of cake and the back door was wide open. Sinson was having a doze on a stone bench by the door. Isora had on a Campofrío apron that the ham distributors had given her. It's not done yet, she said. Her eyes were downcast. Every time Chela put Isora on a diet, she got sad. Then all she'd talk about was food and all the things she wished she could eat and how to make yogurt cake and flan. The kitchen counter was covered in flour and empty tubs of yogurt. Shit, I found this super-awesome thing in a drawer. Lemme show you, she said. Then she took me by the arm to her Tía Chuchi's bedroom, where there was a bas-relief of *The Last Supper* hanging above the headboard. Isora opened a drawer and took out a lighter. On it a man with a willy as big as a sausage dog was leaning against a palm tree next to a woman on a white-sand beach. As Isora moved the lighter around, the man's willy disappeared inside the woman and then appeared again. The lighter had one of those shiny threedee pictures on it. Super-gross, I said. Shit, d'you think my aunt smokes weed? she asked. Dunno, maybe she got it for her birthday. Then Isora put the lighter away because it'd started to smell like there was something burning.

By the time Isora set the cake on the table, I was swallowing hard. The cake was round with a hole in the middle and the top was kind of burnt. Isora told me to eat it while it was still hot, 'cause it's better that way. My ma says that if you eat cake when it's still hot you'll get a tummyache, I said. That's a fib, she jus doesn't want you eatin' it straight away, she wants you to wait till you're hungry. Isora always knew when grown-ups were lying. She served me a slice of cake and I ate it one bite at a time. It wasn't good, it had a baking-soda aftertaste and made me feel like I'd just swallowed a mouthful of pool water with lots of chlorine in it. As I slowly ate the cake, Isora said that a woman from church had told her nan that Isora could lose lots of weight real fast if she ate onion soup for breakfast, lunch and dinner, that it was the disgustingest thing in the world but if she stuck with it she could finally be super-skinny like Rosario from *Pasión*. Isora grabbed the cooking pot with her nan's soup in it and took off the lid to show me what it looked like. There were tons of onions floating in a yellowish liquid like boats adrift at sea. I wished people worried about me getting fat too, I thought. The only person who encouraged me to eat less was Isora, except she stopped caring when she was on a diet because all she wanted was for someone to eat for her. Isora always said we'd be happy as soon as we were as thin as Rosario and allowed to shave our legs, and I thought she was right and that the day they let me wax my moustache would be the happiest day of my life.

Between the stink of the onion soup and the disgustingness of the cake, I got the urge to spit it all out and drink a big glug of water. Instead I held it together and had another bite while Isora watched me eat forkful after forkful of her cake. For her, even the smallest movement was important. She enjoyed watching my fingers travel from the cake to my mouth and kept telling me now eat it like this, now eat it like that, and then staring. When Isora got up to go to the bathroom I ran to the door and said here, Sinson, have some cake, and then fed him the last piece. The dog started huckahuckaing because the cake was bone-dry and his throat was phlegmy from old age. But he ate the entire thing, like when a snake in a documentary gulps down a rabbit in a single bite, because he was used to eating whatever folks gave him. Chela always fed him leftovers, bones and all.

Did it taste good, Shit? Want some more? Isora asked when she came back. Instead of saying no, I nodded. Up and down. She slid another slice on to a napkin and then we went and played with our Barbies. Isora kept checking on the cake. Every time I saw her look at it I'd put down my doll, grab a piece of cake and shove it in my mouth. That day, our Barbies lived on a ranch in Redondo. They had servants whose butts they kicked while they said I don't pay you to fuck around, jackass, now get back to work! As Isora made one of her Barbies kick her only Ken doll, who we pretended was lots of different servants at the same time, I thought about how I could never bring myself to tell her that I didn't like this thing or that thing and how, if she asked me to do something, I always did it, no questions asked, like I was the Ken doll and she was a Barbie kicking my butt.

All the servants had died of starvation and heatstroke by the time Nana called Chela's phone and told me to come home for lunch. I helped Isora collect the Barbies and started heading out the door, but before I could leave Isora yelled Shiiiiiiit, take some cake with you, won't you, and ran after me with two pieces, each in their own napkin. I took them and left without saying a word because I found it so hard to say goodbye. Instead I liked to pretend I wasn't leaving at all. I walked up the road and saw Gaspa near the pond, stinking of piss. Like all the neighbourhood dogs, Gaspa was a donkey-grey mutt with matted fur and teeth that stuck out. I thought of tossing him some cake, but then remembered how Sinson had huckahuckaed and got scared Gaspa might choke to death, seeing as he was so much older than Sinson. I carried on up the steep hill and Gaspa started to follow me. He dragged his two hind legs, as though his body weighed about the same as five bags of concrete. I didn't know who Gaspa belonged to and I suspected nobody wanted him. We passed Melva's house and Gaspa nestled closer and closer to my legs. He stared at my hands like a starved thing. A white dog ran on to the road near Nana's cousin's and came after me too. He was white with a black spot round his right eye. He looked silkier than Gaspa, and younger too. Gaspa was always getting into fights as a pup. But he got softer with age and the other dogs didn't bother him so much any more. Gaspa and Chovi, that's what I called the white dog, walked beside me, their eyes glued on the cake.

We headed on up the hill, and by the time I could see Nana's place from the crossroads I had five dogs on my heels in all colours and sizes. There was Gaspa and Chovi, then two abandoned hunting dogs that showed up on Tuesdays and Thursdays and tore through the trash bags that were left out for the garbage truck, and a tiny, sickly mutt, the ugliest, stinkiest dog I ever saw in my life. They followed me to Nana's front door and I left them out there. A bowl of soup was waiting for me in the kitchen. I didn't like mint, so I picked it out. I swirled the spoon round the bowl for a while, but in the end I didn't eat it. Nana still let me have some salad and a slice of potato tortilla with Libby's tomato sauce because at Nana's you didn't have to finish your plate, you could do whatever you wanted. After lunch, Nana turned on the telenovela on the kitchen TV. I always got yawny around that time of day, but I didn't like sleeping when it was still light out so I never had a nap. I stood up to get a glass of well water from the bucket on the counter by the kitchen window. My ma didn't like me to drink well water because it was untreated, but when it was just me and Nana I did it anyway. I liked it better than Fonteide water and sometimes it gave me the shits, which made me happy because it made Isora happy. I scooped some water with Tío Ovidio's tin cup. I drank with my teeth against the rim. The water slowly squidged through the gaps between my canines. I got on my tiptoes and looked out the window. There they were, a dozen or so dogs lounging at Nana's front door, some sleeping while others scratched at fleas. Up above, the whole sky was a single, heavy black cloud. Looks like rain, I thought. Looks like rain.

Juanita's Hollering Echoed
Past the Crossroads

None of the boys in the neighbourhood liked to play with Barbies or dolls. Except for Juanita Banana, who did whatever we wanted. We always gave him the ugliest Barbie doll with the tackiest clothes, and he'd hold it in his hand like he'd found an ancient treasure and then say, in a chirrup, hiya, myname'sChaxiraxi-andI'mcute. Juanita Banana was always begging us to invite him over to play Barbies because he didn't have any of his own. Juanito's grandad said that boys these days were turning out a bit faggoty, which is why Juanita Banana always brought a football with him when he came over, so that nobody would suspect what we really got up to. Nana didn't care that Juanito played with dolls, sometimes she even joined in too, though her way of playing was different. She scrubbed the muck off the dolls, which were dirty from us grinding them into the mounds of concrete sand outside her house, then left them on the front steps, all cute and stylish and clean as a whistle.

We played marbles with him too. Juanita Banana had more marbles than either of us because boys always got more money for Tazos and marbles than girls did, and we only had four or five of each. Juanita Banana had a beautiful, glittery white marble that me and Isora'd had our eyes on for ages. Isora didn't know how to play marbles, but she made up her own rules. And she was so feisty and stubborn that she always ended up winning. She'd yell gongo!, but it'd be a lie. One day, Juanito got up to pee behind a bush of vinagrera and Isora said gongo, you bastard! And by the time Juanita had rushed over, his trousers all splashed with pee, Isora'd already swiped his glittery white marble, and that was the last we saw of it. Other times, we played on our Gamebois for hours on end. Juanita and me both had the Advance, but Isora was still in charge because her game cartridge was better. Me and Juanita would stand behind Isora and watch her beat each level, looking over her shoulder to see if her character had drowned or caught fire, but Isora never died. Isora made up the rules for every game, even the ones on the Gameboi. Whenever she messed up, she just said that it was her turn again because the game was hers and Juanita and me had our own Gamebois and that was the end of it.

I wanted to play Hamtaro as badly as taters want it to rain.

It was Wednesday, and you could see shreds of the vulcano through the wisps of cloud that drifted between the pines. The cloud cover was thick, but it was windy and every so often the sun peeked through the cracks in the white sky and warmed our shoulders. We were on Nana's front steps. Above us was a big pink bougainvillea vine that I sometimes used to make-believe I lived in a castle with lots of gardens and lions. Juanito was playing with Chaxiraxi, the ugly Barbie doll with the smooshed-in face. Chaxiraxi was wearing a quilt-fabric outfit that Nana made for her after me and Isora set fire to her real clothes because she'd got fresh with us. Me and Isora had our usual Barbie dolls. That day hers was called Jennifer López and mine was Saray, like the girl who dropped turds all over the neighbourhood. Our Barbies were super-cute and wore their hair in perfect ponytails. Chaxiraxi was telling us she had sexed a man behind Bar de Antonio who stank of wine. Isora put JLo's face right up to Saray's and whispered chacha, Chaxi works as a prosty, and Saray went hehehehehehe with one hand over her mouth. Sometimes we were real mean to Chaxi, but Juanita Banana appreciated our jokes and always peed himself laughing. Chaxiraxi started soaring naked above the potted palm trees that Nana'd set on the front steps. Isora was getting aggravated because Juanita Banana was ruining the game again. The realistic stuff was never enough for Juanita. He always wanted to make the Barbies fly, fall off a cliff or breathe fire. ForfuckssakeJuanita, Isora said, either do things how you're s'posed to or we're not gonna let you play! That's when we heard the footsteps on the path and an old, gruff voice, dark as a cave. Juan, come here rightthisminute! It was Juanito's grandad, clutching a belt. He walked right up to where we sat and yanked Chaxiraxi out of his hands. I almost peed myself, I got so scared. Isora said that Juanito was jus helping us set up the Barbies, but that didn't change a thing. His grandad grabbed him by the ear and wrung it like a wet kitchen towel, then dragged him out on the street and into the house. The Barbie doll was left on the ground, legs akimbo. You could see the shadow of the bougainvillea on her naked body. Isora plugged my ears with two of her fingers. And I plugged hers. For a long while we looked each other in the eyes, without moving. I started to hear this loud pounding in my ears, like I had a heart inside my head – budumbudumbudum – and my heartbeat was smacking its fingers against the walls of my body. I focused hard but felt nothing below my fingers. There was no heartbeat. It was like Isora's body had no heart inside it, only guts.

We let go. The sound of Juanita's hollering echoed past the crossroads.

to eat isora

isora had green eyes like the greenest green like a fly
sat on a tuna salad sandwich in august on a beach in
teno like a drained bottle of wine when isora's nan got
mad she'd say i'll drain you through and through i'll
drink your blood rightthisminute you little cunt isora
had round tits that sprang out of her like when the
earth spits up a flower that's small at first then big the
dry earth of her breasts then stretch-marked her tits
didn't fit her skin and she cried isora had pubes on her
minky and sometimes she shaved them all the way
up to her butthole and her butt would itch isora had
thick black pubes like the fake grass round holiday
homes on her minky isora's hair smelled like gofio like
toasted almonds like croutons when i saw isora coming
i felt calm like when i could hear the stew simmering
at noon isora had pudgy fingers and jagged nails like
a goat had chewed on them sometimes i'd watch her

touch things grab hold of a fork stroke the pages of the textbook because it had a strange glossy texture or write in the minimarket ledger and i'd get the urge to squeeze her hand and twist it until all her fingers popped out of their sockets until her hands were just gone sometimes i hated her and wanted to destroy her isora's lips were flush like she'd been smacked on the kisser i'd kiss her on the red bits behind the cultural centre isora was my best friend i wanted to be like her my eyes were brown one darker than the other one lighter than the other and when i was born my ma thought i was blind and ran to ask the doctor i barely had any hair on my minky and ma only let me clip it with a beard trimmer i wanted to shave it all off with my dad's razor but dad wouldn't let me isora would say you're so lucky you haven't got tits and the boys don't laugh shit shit she called me shit jus like that in english because poop was a beautiful thing like the mist round the pines isora said that in the forest there were witches who talked about ma isora talked to herself sometimes and sometimes she slept with her eyes open and she cursed at me in dreams sometimes we'd see each other at three in the morning asleep outside the minimarket and we were like ghosts clinking bones under the moonlight isora looked like a calla lily she was soft like a calla lily she was taller taller than me on top of a crag on top of a crag isora

was moist like a tuberose full shoulders small ears a
mole on her chin a hair on the mole on her chin that
was really small and raised like a bird perched on the
tip of her chin a dimple in her chin like a puddle her
collarbones like thorns her bones spiked at the ends i
liked isora's insides even though i couldn't see them i
thought they must be perfect spheres i liked the underside of her arms white and barbed soft and rough at
the same time isora had a birthmark on her butt she
said it was a lovemark from her ma i liked isora's teeth
the way the bottom row and the top row fit together
a perfect machine perfect pure just about see-through
isora said orgasm and i thought a condom was when
a minky and a willy came together i didn't know the
difference between me and isora sometimes i thought
we were the same girl isora drank leche leche coffee
with regular milk and condensed milk she sucked the
condensed milk up with a straw like grannies did and
i wanted to suck up isora's head so i'd have her inside
my body like the pregnant girl with the lilú doll who
was always on tv big-bellied inside isora's body inside
isora inside kissing my belly inside i wanted to eat
isora and then poop her out so she'd be mine to store
the poop in a box so i could see her whenever i wanted
and i wanted to become her to be isora inside isora
isora isora isora drinking a glass of milk with gofio
and sugar and saying foc yu in mai laif isora knocking

my head with her sneakers isora cracking my head
with her sneakers isora saying shit shut your hole
don't be a moron don't you realize my nan can hear
you

ima tuch u in ways dat havnt
evn been invntd

We had an Aventura song book, Isora and me. Isora always said Aventura was the best band in the whole world, and I thought so too. Whenever I listened to Aventura I got this feeling in my body, like the songs were whisking my insides around with a stick. Uh-huh, that's right, Isora said whenever Romeo sang something we liked. Uh-huh, that's right, and then she'd make me write it down in our SsOoOngG BoOoKkk. We called our notebook a SsOoOngG BoOoKkk because when we'd stolen it from under the minimarket counter, the hard, brown, cloth-bound cover had the word LEDGER stamped on it and Isora said we should tape a piece of white paper over it and give it a new name in up-and-down letters like the ones we used on mésinye. We wrote it out in a sparkly blue pen that always ran dry halfway through a sentence.

Isora had a red MP3 player. It was beautiful and red like a hog plum. She'd got it from her second cousin from Santa Cruz, who always gave her techie things. Isora knew lots about music. Whenever they went to town, her nan gave her money to buy CDs at the guagua station, and she got the rest of the songs from the internet café. Isora knew all of Aventura's songs by heart, and sometimes out of the blue she'd start singing *si me enseñaste a querer, también enséñame a olvidar esto que siento, porque eres tú niña querida la mujer a quien yo amo y a quien quiero, quién sanará este dolor que me dejaste en mi interior cuando te fuistes?, quién inventó el amor debió dar instrucciones pa evitar el sufrimiento.* Then she'd stop and have a quick think and say, Shit, write that down in the SsOoOngG BoOoKkk and I'd write out the line in my own way: *whoever invntd luv shoulda left instrukshons on how 2 not get hurt.*

Aventura's songs were about life's truths. Sometimes me and Isora read out some of the bits we wrote in the SsOoOngG BoOoKkk. We always said that if we stored them in our heads for a while, by the time we grew up we'd know way more about love than anyone. Sometimes, when Isora got caught up in the music, I'd run my finger down the lyrics in the song book and try to commit them to memory:

1) 1 kss = frenship sex & luv ne where in da world no matter da relijon w 1 kss frum her ill fly 2 heven tlk 2 god, tuch the starz
2) wen u lose a luv evrythng bout how u c n feel changes
3) papa sed 2 not cry ovr womn but thats wut i do 4 u
4) as a ladysman 1 luv wuz enuf & now dat im serius i drink down da pain
5) when ur a slave 2 luv ur haAaAarts stompd all ovr cuz if u luv but dont sho it u betta get redi 4 hurt
6) havin sex aint da same as makin luv
7) From Obsesión: sry if i ofend u but i kno dat i m honest lisn 2 da richnss of my version pur creem & choclat 2 rub u w & eat u w & take u 2 nother world corazoOon!!! lets hav an aventura lets do 1,000 lokuras ima tuch u in ways dat havnt evn been invntd

I'd go back to the beginning and run my finger along *lets hav an aventura lets do 1,000 lokuras ima tuch u in ways dat havnt evn been invntd*. Then I'd look at Isora and think about how I couldn't touch her the way other girls touched and hugged, but maybe I could touch her *in ways dat havnt evn been invntd*, stroke the backs of her knees with my hand or run my fingers along the scabs that edged her toenails or rub the rolls of flesh that stuck out over her panties.

Footsteps on the Tarmac

There was just over a month until the neighbourhood fiesta, and I couldn't wait to see the little papers strung in zigzags between each lamp post, all the way from Doña Carmen's house to the tip-top of our street, where the feeling of celebration mixed with the pine trees. That summer the fiesta committee wouldn't quit asking for money. When Nana heard the sound of Pepe Benavente blasting from the car as it came up the road or of the men outside laughing, she'd say here comes the fiesta committee! and I'd rush to turn off the TV and close the shutters. I'd be hiding in the shed before you could say boo, my breath soft and quiet so they'd think we weren't home and wouldn't ask us for money. When we weren't fast enough, because their music was on low or we couldn't hear them approaching, the fiesta committee guys would stand at the front steps and call out Almeriiiiiiiinda, c'mon down! And there was nothing Nana could do but open the door and fork over the handful of money she'd set aside to settle her tab at the minimarket. Other times, if the fiesta committee'd already heard the sound of the TV and Nana only had two sad euros in her wallet, she and Tío Ovidio would crawl into the shed and make me open the door. I'd see the men with their tanned, sweaty heads under straw hats tied with Dorada's red ribbons and the tin money buckets in their hands, and they'd say miniña, go fetch your nana, and I hated lying so much my mouth froze up in panic, and I'd tell them Nana wasn't home and they should come back another time, and before they could say anything else I'd bolt the door.

That afternoon the fiesta committee had hit every house in the neighbourhood and left everyone feeling more washed out than a land crab. I was playing on a rusted bicycle with hard, jaggedy pedals that stabbed my ankles at the junction of my street and Donkey's Pass. Nana came outside and asked if I could fetch her some eggs and cold meats. From where I stood, I could see Isora at the end of the road. I liked to watch as she came closer and feel her footsteps on the tarmac. The whole ground shook. All it took was seeing her there, at the end of the road, at the crest, where the hillside was almost vertical, for me to feel completely happy. Like when you get in the ocean for the first time after lots and lots of years. She kept picking her wedgie, which gave her a limp and made her look like a duck with a ponytail. Shiiiiiiit! she yelled, from all the way down there. And I raised my hand.

We skipped down the road because Isora had got it in her head that it was faster that way. The bad thing about racing downhill like that was it could be real hard to stop. The hill was so steep that our bodies had no choice but to keep going. Near Melva's we bumped into a couple of boys called Ayoze and Mencey, who were both younger than us but clever. They were play-ing footy and had to chase after the ball, which kept getting away from them, sometimes rolling as far as the church. That day they were playing ball on the street, but most of the time they played at La Güerta School Footy Club, a rough-and-ready football pitch in one of the fields behind the pond. Everything in the neighbourhood was at a slant, and the same went for La Güerta School Footy Club. The boys had tried to level the pitch with pine needles and rocks, but then it rained and it all went to hell anyhow. After a lot of unfairness, they decided the lower-down team's goals would count for double. Wanna play butt-tag? the boys asked when they saw us skipping down the road. I stopped, but Isora carried on and from way down the hill she told them no, that we were gonna do our own thing. I loved how easy it was for Isora to say no.

She wasn't scared that people would stop liking her. She said what she wanted when she wanted. I turned round and flew after her, scared the boys would kick the ball at us for being snooty, and when I caught up with her I slammed my sneakers into the tarmac and stopped. Isora picked her wedgie again. Suffocating, breathless and red in the face, she said Shit, you ever seen Sinson with his willy out? Doesn't it look like a tube of red lipstick?

Super-skinny Like a Hunting Dog

Nana's loquats
bouquets of sourgrass
pictures of exploding vulcanos
figs
taters pinched from the fields
yellow and purple plums
mulberry leaves for silkworms (if they had
    silkworms)
old Babybjörn clothes for the lilbabies
saint's candles
saint's stamps
prickly pears in wicker baskets
chorizo sausage sarnies
water from the well
pinched parsley
roadside almonds
Isora's yogurt cake

Isora's chocolate cake (when it turned out good)
the HiperDino coupon magazines
pictures of the vulcano dressed as a wizard
pictures of small kids dressed as wizards
pinched bananas
pictures of bananas dressed as wizards dancing
    atop the vulcano
made-up things about the Canary Islands that
    tourists thought were cool

These were the things me and Isora wanted to sell so she could get a gutstric balloon, as she called it. A gutstric balloon. Because she'd heard at the minimarket – and there was lots to hear at the mini-market – that there was a woman who lived below the church – and I didn't have a clue where she meant, because everything below the church was a mystery to me – who had a gutstric balloon put in and went from weighing two hundred kilos to being super-skinny like a hunting dog. She said she'd heard it at the market early that morning while helping her nan stock the shelves, and that she was so discomboobulated by the news that she dropped a tin of corned beef and Chela yelled watch it, butterfingers! You're not all there, are you? I bet you've got something missing in the head. She picked the can up from the floor and that's when it dawned on her, that's when the idea came into her head that if we saved up enough money in the piggy bank for a pair of gutstric balloons we'd be super-skinny for the rest of time, and la bitch would never put her on another onion diet or pineapple diet or lime juice diet or apple juice diet ever again.

We got hold of some of the stuff on our list. Nana's loquats, bouquets of sourgrass, pictures of the exploding vulcano made by Isora, figs, saint's candles that we pinched from Nana's shed, prickly pears that Tío Ovi picked for us by climbing up into the cactus and knocking the pears off with a broom, which he used to brush off all the spines, though he always wound up prickled all over anyhow, even on his eyelids. We also got bunches of roadside parsley and pictures of the vulcano dressed as a wizard and of kids dressed as wizards and of bananas dressed as wizards dancing atop the vulcano, all of them made by Isora, who signed the bottom of every drawing BY ISORA like she was a big-time artist. And we got hold of some HiperDino coupon magazines as well, mostly we got HiperDino magazines, which we found in Tío Ovi's room in a massive stack next to another stack of *¡Hola!* magazines, which were all about famous people whose names Isora knew while I didn't.

The first place we tried with our HiperDino magazines and bouquets of sourgrass was the holiday homes, but then the gardening man opened the door and saw the junk we'd brought with us and said what the devil have you got there, ain't nothing but rubbish, and he told us to clear off, go home, scat. Isora had the idea that we should stand at the crossroads, in case any of the foreners drove up in their cars, and yell tipical canari islan while pointing at the prickly pears and at the HiperDino magazines, and we bet our booties they were dumb enough to buy something. After half an hour of standing at the crossroads next to a huge rock we'd hauled over from a field, where we arranged some of our made-up canari-islan wares, Isora said Shit, I'm bored, let's hit the road. We headed down to the central part of the neighbourhood, the one between the gayhouse and Doña Carmen's, which I'd always thought of as the area where the rich folks lived, the ones from the neighbourhood association and from the fiesta committee, and I'd always wanted to live right by Isora so that I could be near the cultural centre and Bar de Antonio and the church square, and the little committee room. And Chela started yelling at us from afar, what junk have you got there, huh? And with her lips pursed and a glare in her eyes, Isora whispered eat caca you foquin bitch.

When we reached the bar, Isora said we should prolly jus head straight to Doña Carmen's, she didn't feel like going inside Bar de Antonio. We started singing Aventura's 'La boda'. When I get married,

Shit, my dress'll be so long everybody's gonna trip on it on their way into church, she said out of the blue. When we got to Doña Carmen's, *La mujer en el espejo* was playing on the TV. Not on TV-TV but on a tape that Doña Carmen's son, who'd moved to Los Silos to be with his girlfriend, had made for her one day while he was visiting, and that Doña Carmen liked to put on every now and then – to feel something, she said. Doña Carmen was doing the dishes and listening to the telenovela as we snuck in like a pair of dogs about to start sniffing around. We dumped all our wares on the kitchen table. Ah no miniña, I haven't two pennies to rub together, a glum Doña Carmen told Isora. Are you hungry, misniñas? How's about I whip up some eggs and fries? I've got some gorgeous taters on hand, the small kind. Yeah, I'd have a teeny bit, Isora said.

In the end we ate so much I had to undo my jeans just to breathe. Doña Carmen collected our plates, which were spotless because we'd even licked up the yolky bits of the eggs. Doña Carmen's plates were just like Nana's, white with a green and yellow border, the ones you got for free if you bought lots of ham. Shit, it hurts like crazy right here, Isora whispered. She whispered and pointed at the pit of her stomach. Doña Carmen was talking to herself about Lanegrita, a hen she had that wouldn't lay eggs. Isora went straight to the bathroom. I sat frozen in my chair. I looked at

Doña Carmen. Her shoes were full of holes and her sweatpants, sweater and apron were bleach-stained and smeared in goat cack. She wore her white hair up in a bun and a green Piensos González León hat. Doña Carmen was someplace else, and for a second I wished I was in that other place too. People said she lost her mind when her husband fell off the scaffold and smashed to pieces like a rabbit. Like a rabbit with all its insides hanging out. I heard the toilet flush in the bathroom. And I thought of how my ma was always asking me: if Isora went and jumped off a cliff, would you jump too? Isora came back to the kitchen and sat at the table. Her clothes were all wet and her hair was a mess. Miniña, aren't you cold? Doña Carmen asked her. I always look like I'm under the weather, all day bundled up in more layers than skin. Isora was breathing heavily and rubbing her hands on her wet clothes. Her eyes were green, like green grapes that've been tossed out. She was in a whole other world too, a place like the one Doña Carmen had gone to. And there I was, sitting in that chair with a belly full of eggs and fries as I watched Isora shudder like a poisoned mouse.

Grinding

On the schoolroom chair, just like that, the way animals grind on poop and decomposing frogs, just like that we grinded on the schoolroom chairs. All the kids were sitting in class, and the class was small, and there was a single teacher for two grades. You had first years on the left-hand side and second years on the right-hand side, and the teacher taught each of us a teeny bit and then we sat around and listened to him teach the older kids. Which is why we learned faster and why we could divide numbers with three digits, and why we grinded on our chairs, like hogs in manure, like hogs in horse manure. Then we all stank of minkies, the whole class stank of minkies and the kids' clothes stank of minkies too, as did the teacher and the teacher's hands, from touching the same piece of chalk that we did.

The table shook like those earthquakes that come before a vulcanic eruption, even though there was never an eruption, even though the vulcano never ever exploded. Like when the mayor went on TV and said quiet down, everyone, quiet down, because there were all these earthquakes making the whole world shake and we were scared to death an eruption would get us. I figured that if the vulcano blew up we could steal a boat from San Marcos beach and sail over to La Gomera.

Like that, when the table shook like an earthquake, when the table shook like those earthquakes that come before a vulcanic eruption, that's how I knew Isora was grinding on her chair. So I copied and started grinding too.

At first we only grinded once in a while, and always in secret. But after we found out the vulcano might explode, we started grinding harder and more often. And we talked about grinding all the time. We were gonna die, so we might as well do as much grinding as we could.

We'd been grinding on things ever since we were small. In the summer, when there wasn't much to do, we grinded more and more often. We used clothes pegs to touch ourselves over the cut-off sweatshorts we wore in the summer. When we drew, we slipped crayons under our panties and when we played with Babybjörns we slipped the dolls under too. We touched ourselves with Barbie heads and with Barbie hair and then everything smelled of minky, of those itsy crabs that skitter across the rocks, of salt water that dries in puddles and forms a gross crust that's hard like a slab of concrete. Sometimes we got marker stains all over our clothes and our pens would explode, but we carried on grinding and grinding until we'd finished, we always held out until we finished. Then we'd have to come up with an excuse to give our mothers, which is when Isora would remember that she didn't have a mother, though she knew that if her mother ever saw her like that she'd throw up.

Isora always made me pray when we finished grinding and I went psspsspsspss with my sweat-shorts streaked in colours, like a rainbow between my thighs, like a rainbow that rose up above the ocean, all the way down there, where the clouds mixed with the sea and everything was grey, and then it was just our minkies left, throbbing like a pair of blackbird hearts buried in the earth, like a forest about to burst into flower in the centre of the Earth.

My Saint with Scraped Knees

When the telenovela ended and the clouds smashed into the tops of our foreheads, a strange and distant sadness would flood Isora, a sadness that was like the whack of a hammer or the piquipiqui of a woodpecker. Then Isora would say I want to take my life, I want to die. She said it just like that, in those words, as if she was a woman of fifty instead of a girl of ten.

We'd run and run, our legs naked. Through the nettles and milk thistles and cactuses. We'd run and scramble up plum trees, pear trees and apple trees whose tart, green apples stung the roofs of our mouths. Aborted loquats covered the ground. When we were sad, we ate unripe berries and hot pears until they gave us the shits. Shits, shits, shits, we always wanted the shits. We pulled spiderwebs off our faces with the tips of our tongues. We touched minkies by accident. We grinded.

There was sadness, and there was sticking our fingers up our butts. Sadness, and sticking the garden hose up our butts, spritzing our butts like pumpkin patches. Sticking the garden hose up our butts so we'd have to take a dump, so it would be faster and feel better too, so we'd be skinny, skinnier than beanpoles.

When me and Isora cried, we spun in circles until it made us dizzy. We held each other by the shoulders, fell on the ground and got scrapes all over our hands, elbows and shins. Then we'd lick up the blood, like the time when Grandpa told me about how Saint Anthony had a dog that healed his wounds when he was about to die. That was before Grandpa left Nana for the German lady, never to be seen again. I dreamed of healing Isora's sadness, I wanted to be her dog and I wanted her to be my saint with scraped knees.

One time me and Isora went to a fiesta for Saint Anthony in the El Amparo neighbourhood. Nobody'd agree to lend us a dog that we could take with us and the strays refused to be picked up, so Isora said we should bring a cat. We grabbed one of Nana's half-feral cats and tied a rope round its neck. The square was overrun with parakeets, mules, horses, ferrets and goats with huge titties that scraped the floor. Guys vroomed past on motorbikes that sounded like the buzzing of a million flies, and all of a sudden the cat spooked and started jumping all over the town square

ANDREA ABREU

walls. The rope stopped the oxygen from reaching the cat's brain and its eyes popped out of their sockets.

On days when Isora wanted to die I felt like I wanted to die too. According to Isora, the best way to do it was to fill the bathtub all the way to the top with hot water and then slash your wrists. Sometimes I wondered how she knew so much stuff I didn't know, and then I got sad because I didn't have a sadness of my own – my sadness was the same as Isora's except inside my body. It was kind of like a fake sadness, like two copies of the same sadness, like a knock-off sadness. That was me. I had no real reason to be sad, so I just made one up.

Sometimes Isora went real quiet when she got sad. She wouldn't say a word for hours. She'd just sit in a corner of the room under the minimarket, right where the walls touched, and stare into the middle distance. Her eyes were like two splodges, like two bottle flies whirring in a room that stank of wine. Even though it bored me stiff, I always sat next to her and listened to her silence. Like when the men watch the football and their wives watch it with them, even though they couldn't care less, because their husbands are feeling down on life and on work in the South, and the women have no choice but to be there for them because it's their duty.

Jesus's Little Head

Isora's house had two storeys. The top was where they used to live. The bottom was a large room that was turned into a second living space. They only started using the new place after Isora's mother killed herself. The top floor was covered in a layer of dust that made everything look twice as big. Chela didn't like us poking around upstairs, she wanted everything to stay the same as when her daughter was found. There were still used panties in one of the drawers in Isora's mother's bedroom. Sometimes Isora pulled them out and looked at them and touched them and took them on a walk around the rooms. We'd pretend that the panties were from the El 99 store in town, and I'd say what size are you looking for, and is it a gift, and I'm sorry, miniña, but I'm afraid we haven't got any wrapping paper. One day when she pulled out the panties, Isora asked me if I wanted to do something. What kind of something, I asked. Something with the panties, she said. It always scared me when she took out her mother's panties because I knew that if her nan found out she'd crack us both on the heads. Isora said let's each wear a pair of Ma's panties. Please? I didn't think twice. The two of us stood there, naked like a pair of wild beasts, then slipped them on. On her they sort of fitted, but on me they fell all the way down to my ankles. She said go on, get on the bed, but I was scared to because I didn't know if dead folks liked it when you got on their beds, much less while wearing a pair of their panties. But I lay down anyhow and the headboard, which had an engraving of Jesus's little head on it, bounced against the wall and then bounced again when Isora got on top of me. The weight of her boobs pressed into me, and I got this warm feeling in my lower bits, like when there's a stew on the boil and water starts spitting out of the cooking pot. We rolled on the bed, this way and that, hugging, like two cats having a scrap in the middle of the night. We'd roll all the way to the right, to the very end of the bed, and then all the way to the left. We hugged the whole time, even though we weren't the kind of friends who did that kind of thing. Suddenly, we stopped. I was on top. Then, without thinking, I rubbed my panties on hers. And she rubbed her panties against mine. My breath caught in my chest. For a second, I had this thought – that I was her mother and she was the forty-kilo baby who'd torn me in half when I'd given birth to her. All I wanted was to protect her. To take care of her and feed her warm gofio and warm milk from a bottle. I stared into her eyes. Isora looked away. She said c'mon Shit, let's head downstairs before la bitch flips her lid.

Just Meat and Cabbage Stew

At Isora's they ate lots of stuff mixed together. Yellow rice with chicken and sauce with a side of salted fish or taters and eggs or taters and onion repurposed from yesterday's stewed taters, or a side of chickpea and meat stew or watercress stew with taters and meat, all of it scrambled together. At Isora's they ate lots of stuff mixed together, but not that day. That day it was just meat and cabbage stew. The streetlight came in through the red-and-white chequered curtains hanging over the small window of Chela's kitchen, and now and then you could hear Sinson barking at the cars that drove up through the neighbourhood every once in a million years. The meat and cabbage stew sat on the table with steam rolling off it. I wasn't a big fan of meat and cabbage stew, specially when it was sprinkled with gofio. But Isora loved it, and if she sprinkled gofio on her stew then I did the same. Chela's place was nothing like Nana's. We had to finish every last drop of food and scrape the very bottoms of our bowls, and if we left even the teensiest scrap, Chela'd spoon the food down our throats, no matter how cold it was, and slam her hand on the hardwood table, which sounded like an earthquake, and say nobody leaves this table till all of this here is gone, and I won't hear a word outta either of you. Chela always gave Isora a smaller bowl than me because, according to her, Isora ate like a horse and if Chela didn't stay on top of her the girl's appetite got out of control. Isora inhaled her stew and then watched me eat mine. I looked miserable as sin from being made to eat stew that was cold and gloopy because of all the gofio I'd heaped on it to mask the flavour, and on top of that I had to drink buckets of water to keep from choking.

As soon as I finished the stew, I needed the bathroom so bad I thought I'd crap my pants. It felt like I had five bags of concrete sitting in my guts. But I enjoyed holding it in, specially when we played Barbies. It made me happy to feel the pressure on my lower back. That day we played a game with the Barbies that lasted five hours. One thing led to another, and before you knew it the Barbies had had twenty children with various men, and they all wound up killing each other in different ways. Fallen off a cliff, splatted against a rabbit cage, strangled by their own siblings, burned to a crisp because the Barbies had left the taters on the stove top, starved to death. When me and Isora played with our Barbies we copied the telenovelas we watched and the Aventura songs we listened to, which is why bad stuff always happened to them.

We'd been playing for a long time, and it got to the point where I couldn't take the pressure any more. But I decided to hold it in a tiny bit longer, until the game had almost ended. Iso, I said, I need to take a dump. And Iso said that her nan didn't let anyone but them do number two in the bathroom. When Isora said that kind of thing I never knew if she was testing me or if she was telling the truth. But Iso, I'm about to crap my jeans, I said again. She started to think the way old folk do and then popped downstairs, leaving me in a corner of the room with a turd poking out of my hole and smudging my white panties, the ones with blue daisies on them. She came back upstairs carrying an empty box of liquorice, the kind that comes in lots of colours, like an empty rainbow. Go here, she said. In this tiny thing? I asked. And she said yeah, what's the big deal? I couldn't hold it in any longer so I pulled down my panties and squatted over the box of liquorice. Isora watched me with a very serious look on her face, like we were doing something super-important that no one had explained to me. Our Barbies were scattered all over the patio and the armchair, lying on the tables and on top of the Ken dolls, rammed into the plastic palm tree in the corner. In their world, in the world of the Barbies, I was a giant monster taking a poo in a box of liquorice. I pulled up my panties and realized they were covered in caca – or nicotine stains, as Dad called them. Look, Iso, I said, and she told me don't worry about it, Shit, I'll get you a pad. She went to the bathroom and brought me back a wad of toilet paper. Line your panties the way I do when I'm on my period, except near your butt. I followed her instructions without thinking. Isora shut the box with the smelly jumbo turd inside it and then hid the whole thing behind the fridgerators beneath the minimarket, near the chicken wings and the prawns, where nobody could find it.

It was early August. It'd been a week or so since the liquorice turd incident. Even though class had ended forever ago, I'd only filled two pages of my summer-break notebook. Isora was almost done with hers. The sun hadn't come out once since we'd stopped going to school. The clouds were like a latch on the sky, an old latch that was rusted shut. Me and Isora were playing outside the market on her bike while Sinson and Gaspa did the nasty, as Ma called it, and every now and then Chela splashed them with water to put out the fire burning inside them. Chela'd been in the minimarket all morning saying what the Christ

is that smell, something musta gone and died somewhere, and as the customers waited for Chuchi to slice
them a smidge of ham and a smidge of cheese, they
started to feel disgusted too and said fos, there's an
awful stink in here. What in the living hell is that
smell, Chela?

At some point Chuchi went downstairs for some
chicken wings, the kind Nana fried and served with
runny mojo. Soon enough she was running back up
to the market, screaming that the smell of death was
coming from the fucking fridgerators. Chela ran down
to have a look. I'll skin you alive, you little cunt! I'll
drain you! I'll drink your blood! Chela yelled as she
stomped upstairs with the box of turd. Isora was on
the bike. She got off and dropped it right there, in the
middle of the street. Go home, she said. La bitch is
chompin' at the bit today. And since Chela scared the
living daylights out of me, I turned round and legged
it back to my house.

That same night, while me and Nana watched *En
clave de Ja* on the kitchen TV, the phone rang. It was
Isora. I'm grounded, Shit. I've gotta work at the minimarket tomorrow and the day after. La bitch put me on
a diet again, she said the turd was as big as a donkey's
and that I eat too much. But it was my turd, I said. I
know, she said. But I'm better at handlin' la bitch than
you are. And she hung up. Nana was peeling taters for

the following day, and from the window you could see fireworks exploding in the sky. There was probably a fiesta on in one of the neighbourhoods. The fireworks were like giant stars shivering in the black sky.

iso_pinki_10@hotmail.com

That summer, Isora and me signed up for computer classes at the cultural centre. In fairness, we signed up because we wanted to chat on mésinye. There was never any room for us in the afternoons because the kinkis hogged all the computers and you could hardly squeeze inside, because for every kinki at a computer there were three hovering behind him. When we took computer classes we could spend as long as we wanted on the computers. Classes were on Tuesday and Thursday mornings, and we could always skip one or two because the teacher never minded that we weren't there. Mothers sent their lilkids to that class so they'd learn to use computers, which is why me and Isora were studying with a bunch of girls and boys who didn't have mésinye accounts. In fairness, we only went to computer class to fool around. We pretended to pay attention to the teacher, but nothing sank in. The teacher was a man in a navy-blue button-down shirt covered in sweat stains. The poor thing was always overheated no matter the weather, and he went around braying like a donkey, hee-haw, he said, it's hotter than blazes, he said. The computer teacher spat when he talked. He was tubby and loved playing chequers and chess. I didn't like people who played chess because I didn't understand it and that made me suspicious. The computer teacher's favourite thing was to make us design borders in Word. His least favourite thing, which we knew because he never shut up about it, was trouble. I'm a peaceful guy, he always said, and I don't like trouble. The man's as patient as Job, as Nana put it. Even though he knew me and Isora slapped together a border in under five seconds and then signed on to mésinye, he never brought it up. If he ever saw mésinye open on our computer, he played dumb and carried on teaching the littler kids about Word. In March or so of that year, back when the computers had just arrived at the cultural centre, Bar-de-Antonio Antonio's daughter Zuleyma helped all of us open mésinye accounts. Isora got hers on the first day. I got mine on the second because I needed to ask my parents for permission, and they always came home from work so late I was almost sound asleep in front of the TV with Nana. Isora always did stuff without asking, in part because her nan never knew what went on in her life, and in part because Isora didn't care if she did dangerous stuff without telling the grown-ups, because Isora had a minimarket and that made her famous and famous people could get away with murder.

Isora's account was iso_pinki_10@hotmail.com and it was way cooler than mine. She was better at it too. I always shared a computer with Isora in class because, to be honest, I didn't totally understand those thingamabobs. One day Acaymo, a kinki, showed Isora how to chat with people in other places, and she never forgot. Meanwhile, I just stared at the computer like when cats will sometimes stare at Nana when she fries chicken. I liked what I saw but had no idea what she was doing.

That day, when the computer teacher wandered off, Isora signed into a Terra chat room with iso_pinki_10@hotmail.com. Suddenly lots and lots of mésinye requests started popping onscreen. So many that the computer froze. I was nervous the teacher would find out, but Isora just laughed and whispered don't be lame, Shit, and then started clicking open some of the windows, but only the ones she was interested in, because what I thought didn't matter. She started chatting.

Isoritatuputita: ola

carlossion: sup?

Isoritatuputita: nm, u?

carlossion: nm, it's hooooot af here ;)

Tell him you've gotta go bottom burp and that you'll be right back, I suggested. But she ignored me and carried on typing.

Isoritatuputita: totes, hot af jus lyk my pussy is rn

carlossion: lol rly? Im hot 2

Isoritatuputita: wher u from?

carlossion: mostoles, u?

Chos, where's that? I asked Isora. I think it's near Médano, she said. Yeah, near Médano. Hey, ask him if he's a stupid centipede boy or what. She ignored me again.

Isoritatuputita: the south

carlossion: how old r u?

Isoritatuputita: 25 & im rly drty

carlossion: u got a cam?

Isoritatuputita: yea, ill do mine if u do urs

carlossion: ok

Isoritatuputita: ok

We didn't have a cam, but he did. In the small square where before we could see a photograph of carlossion's motocross bike there was now a ginormous willy that looked kind of like a chocolate-filled pachanga sprinkled all over with sugar. It was purple and veiny, and I'd never seen anything like it. Isora was pissing herself laughing, even though I knew she was actually a little scared. I tried to cover the screen and kept telling Isora to make it go away because the teacher was starting to look cross.

carlossion: u lyk it putita?

Before we could do anything about it, the teacher turned towards us and then came up to our computer.

carlossion: im hard jus 4 u ;)

The teacher was sweaty all over like a black hog. When he saw carlossion's ginormous willy on the screen he went red, tomato-red, as Nana called it, red with rage because he was a peaceful guy who didn't like trouble and we'd worn the poor man out.

carlossion: u there?

carlossion: u lyk it?

All the littler girls and boys looked terrified as they turned to stare at the computer. The teacher took us to the door and said we were banned for the rest of the week. I cried and begged him not to tell Nana. Even though Isora was still laughing as we left, I was raging at her. She walked me to Nana's and I didn't say a word the whole way. It was nearly lunchtime. The sky was a solid sheet of grey – nothing but clouds, clouds dark as night. While we sat at the kitchen table, a plate of spaghetti with meat sauce in front of us, it started drizzling. I watched the raindrops hit the windowpane and felt a knot at the pit of my stomach. Jesus, won't you look at that disgusting fog, Nana said. This isn't summer, it's not anything, said Isora.

carlossion: ola??

To the Soundtrack of Pepe Benavente

I think he's having an orgasm, said Juanita Banana. Who? I asked. The priest, he said. Huh, what makes you think that? I shot back. Because Julio (Juanito never said the word dad and always called his pops by his first name) says that when you love a woman very much you have an orgasm, and that it can get her pregnant. Don't be stupid, Juanito, said Isora, that's when they're fucking, not when they're in love. And when Isora said the word fuck the bottoms of my feet tingled. All day we'd played in a field behind the church, across from Doña Carmen's and right next to the room where the committee met to count the money they'd squeezed out of everyone in the neighbourhood and discuss the programme for the fiesta and grill meat and drink wine – all of it to the soundtrack of Pepe Benavente. It was extra-foggy out. Doña Carmen was sitting on a rock outside her house in a sunhat, watching a dog piss and drop turds on the plants by her front door and on the wild dill daisies that grew in the abandoned garden beds and on the sourgrass that lined the walls, which is why my ma said I mustn't ever eat any of the sourgrass I found on the street, because it was splashed in dog pee. All afternoon we'd played a game called lazybones that Juanita Banana had made up. Me and Isora were the parents – she was the mother and I was the father – of a fifteen-year-old boy who did nothing but watch dirty movies, drink strawberry soda pop and laze around all day. We spent the whole time arguing with the no-good bum, who was kicked back on a bale of hay listening to 'El Polvorete' play on the committee room speakers on repeat, until the fog grew so thick and cold we had to go home. We had on flip-flops and shorts and walked out of the field covered in burrs, the soles of our feet chalkboard-black. As we passed the committee room, Isora decided to go in and ask the president – a man named Tito with a belly as big as a boulder and a round outie that looked like an avocado stone popped right in the middle – if they could please bring Tony Tun Tun to the fiesta this year, because Redondo had got him last year and, well, our neighbourhood deserved him too. First let's see if we've got enough do-re-mi to make it work, Tito said. And if it's not him it'll be somebody else, miniña. Then he handed us each a hunk of meat and a roll of bread. Juanita walked on the pavement all the way up to the church with a spring in his step, the two of us trailing behind him. When we reached the banisters that separated the street from the square, I saw a familiar look in Isora's eyes. Somebody was dry-humping near us, and whenever any dry-humping went on, Isora got a twinkle in her eye and a sparkly look on her face. Chos, said Isora, I wonder who those hornballs are. We tiptoed up to the banisters and peeked through the gap. We realized straight away that the hornball was Isora's Tía Chuchi, though we couldn't make out who she was hornballing. After a while, as the two of them carried on smacking lips, we saw his face. It was Damián, the altar server from El Amparo. Damián was at least six years younger than Chuchi, and Isora laughed at him all the time because she said that the reason he wanted to become a priest was that he had a small willy, and the reason she knew that was because la bitch was always saying that priests were a bunch of little willies.

Juanito stood there pale and quiet, and then after a while he yelled aaaaaah, you're right, you don't get orgasms from kissing! I couldn't remember, but I do now and you're right. And as he said this he slapped his legs. Shhht, chacho, shut up, Juanito, said Isora. They're gonna hear you and think we're spyin' on 'em.

Juanito pretended to lock his lips with his fingers and toss the fake key down his butt crack. And I said, aaach, you're so over the top! Ew, you just ninja-farted, he shot back. Then Isora went on about how Zuleyma from Bar de Antonio had said that after women have sex, their pussies go on throbbing. She said *pussies* instead of *minkies* and I felt a whole world apart from her. Her words squeezed through my throat and it hurt like I was choking, like I'd swallowed food down the wrong tube, the old tube, as Nana called it. Isora was somewhere else, I realized, somewhere I couldn't even see the beginning of, and for a second I felt scared. Scared she'd realize how innocent I was or that she'd get tired of me nodding my head and keeping my mouth shut. Hey, y'know what my brother Goyo told me? Juanito asked. Isora stared at Father Damián and Tía Chuchi as they pawed at each other. He told me that high-school boys hang their sweaters in front of their desks so no one'll see them jerking off. Eww, that's gross, said Isora. And he said that when a guy winks at a girl, that means he's thinking bout her. Isora looked at her aunt and picked her wedgie. All of a sudden she became antsy and said let's get outta here. Then she walked up the road, chewing the rest of her meat.

At the minimarket, Isora asked Chela to make us each a sarnie with sliced chorizo and Merican cheese.

She handed them to us and then Juanita waved good-bye to Isora. I didn't say anything, because it made me sad to leave them. I walked straight out of the market with the sarnie in my hand. Juanita followed. We walked home along the side of the road and raindrops fell from the sky. Juanita wouldn't stop repeating we'll catch cold from this drizzle, we'll catch cold from this drizzle, like an eighty-year-old grannie. Suddenly, I had an image of him in my head. He was grown up and working on a tomato farm in the South. His head was almost completely bald and one of his teeth was black. I pictured him with a group of men making fun of him as he looked sad and said bundle up, misniños, you'll catch cold from this drizzle. Over and over, like an eighty-year-old woman, like a grannie.

Eyes Black Like a Blackbird's Feathers

It was Candelaria Day and the calima was thick. Above, the sky was pure cloud and dust. Sometimes I thought all the dust floating in the air was our fault: a dark, cloudy blanket stoppered the sky, trapping our breaths down below, and the air grew muggier and muggier until it smothered us. It was Candelaria Day, Isora's favourite, the day of her Virgen Morenita, the day of the saint she wore round her neck and stuffed in her mouth and sucked and sucked on all the time. I picked a bouquet of bright-yellow sourgrass from outside Nana's house and went to meet Isora at sun-up. There was almost none left because the sourgrass dried out as summer wore on and you had to wait until winter for it to be yellow and beautiful again and so you could suckle on the sourgrass like a goat kid on its goat mama's titties, mwa mwa, extra-fresh.

I gave Isora the bouquet of sourgrass and wished her a happy name day, then said that Saray had phoned Nana's to ask if we wanted to play in her pool. Saray had a giant plastic swimming pool. Her dad set it up in the field by their house, which belonged to no one. They filled it with water from the well at the start of summer and tossed in some chlorine now and then that they got from Gracían – the one with the bushy eyebrows like butterfly caterpillars, who cleaned pools at a hotel in the South – and as summer marched on, the swimming pool turned green, green and swampy, and became covered in algae and filled with dead bugs and wrigglers that started off small but then grew big like rock gobies in tide pools.

Me and Isora loved swimming in Saray's pool, but we only went if she invited us. Saray's house wasn't like the minimarket, where you could show up whenever you pleased. When we went over to play Help, I'm Drowning!, which was our favourite game to play in the swimming pool, one of us would be the person drowning and the other two would be lifeguards. The person drowning had to hold her breath below water until she was light-headed in real life, and that's when the lifeguards came to rescue her. I never liked being the person drowning, to be honest, because there were times when I took it too seriously and held my breath until my head started pounding like a drum and it hurt like hell, to be honest. Plus, if I spent too long underwater my face went green from the algae and then Nana got cross with me.

Another reason we liked to go over to Saray's was because her parents ran a bar in El Amparo. A sandwich bar. By the time they got home after closing, the three of us would be sleepy and starving hungry. But they always brought back sarnies and loaded fries. That's why we always stayed over late, so that we could eat sarnies and fries criss-crossed with lots of colourful sauces. Isora's favourite was the cruhsant sarnie with egg, pork loin, cheese and salad and mine was the cheese and shredded-beef sarnie. They always brought home a ham and cheese arepa for Saray because Ma said she had a sensitive stomach, the poor thing, and her tummy was messed up from all the bar food she ate, which is why Isora was convinced Saray was the one cacking all over the neighbourhood, not the witches from Donkey's Pass. After eating our sarnies, me and Isora always wound up feeling stuffed as bedbugs and Isora would puke in a corner of the field with the pool in it nearly every time – hucka-huckahucka, she went, like a phlegmy dog.

Dad said that Saray was a bit strange because her parents treated her like a baby. She was two years older than us, even though sometimes she gave the impression that she was four years younger. I got along better with Saray than Isora did. I went over to her house more often and I knew her better too, but that was mostly because Saray lived around the corner from me. Nearly everyone liked Isora more than they liked me: Isora was cleverer and gutsier, she had a way with words and was quick on her feet. She knew how to talk with old people and with young people too. I didn't, though. Saray was the only person on Earth who liked me more.

Saray was being clingier than usual that day. When we played Help, I'm Drowning! she kept wanting the two of us to be the lifeguards and for Isora to be the person drowning, which Isora didn't like one bit. She went along with it twice because she didn't have a choice, because even though she was used to being in charge, we were at Saray's house and in her swimming pool, even if they weren't strictly hers – her family rented the land. The second time Isora played the person drowning, she climbed out of the pool fuming, her face green with algae. She looked like a rotted, ticked-off fish. Fuck this! I'm not fake drowning for you bitches ever again, said Isora, practically howling. Okay, okay, okaaaaaay said Saray. Then let's play models. Models was a game Saray had made up. In it one person got to be the super-pretty model for the day, which meant putting on Saray's mother's clothes and make-up and strutting down their staircase,

which we loved to pieces because it was spiral. Me
and Isora dreamed of having a spiral staircase when
we were all grown up and lived together in the same
house with our two husbands.

We climbed out of the pool and ran into Saray's
house just the way we were, dripping-wet and without
flip-flops on, then sprinted up the spiral staircase to
the master bedroom. Saray opened the bottom drawer
of her mother's dresser. Inside were lots of dresses
made of satin and sparkles and sequins and fringes,
all from when Saray's mother had been young and
worked in hotels in the South as a magician's assist-
ant, which is why Saray always went round telling
people that her ma was famous. By the time Saray
pulled out her mother's sexiest dresses, Isora was
already chewing on her Virgen de Candelaria chain.
Saray dumped the clothes on the fuchsia satin duvet
covering the king-sized bed and turned to face us.
And today's super-pretty model iiiiiiiis . . . you. She
pointed at me. That's when I got extra-nervous, because what I wanted most of all was for Isora to be
the super-pretty model, because I knew she'd hate the
fact that Saray had picked me after what happened
in the pool. Pfffft, are you for real? It's my name day,
fuckssake. I'm done with you selfish bitches. It's jus
not right, Isora said, eyes bulging with anger. Then
she went into the bathroom off the master bedroom

and slammed the door. Now sit down so I can do your make-up, said Saray. Paralysed with fear, I sat down at her mother's dressing table and let Saray have her way.

After painting my face with every colour in the make-up bag and making me try on, like, six different dresses, Saray said I could leave, she was tired and needed to get some sleep. I didn't understand how a full-grown girl could sleep in the middle of the day like a three-month-old baby, but I did what she said. I took off the clothes and knocked on the bathroom door. Iso, c'mout, Saray wants to sleep. Aren't we stayin' for sarnies? she asked from behind the wooden door. No, Saray says she's gotta sleep. Isora opened the door and walked straight down the spiral stair-case. I followed. A small mirror hung in the entryway of Saray's house. I looked terrible. My lips were huge and deformed and my eyes black like a blackbird's feathers. I ran up to Isora, face all covered in splodges. She looked at me and said I wish Saray'd painted my face like that for my name day. She seemed calmer, strange, maybe sad. Her eyes were glazed. Her gold chain hung from the corner of her bottom lip and tugged so hard on her neck it almost cut into the skin. The whole way, she stared down at the tarmac and punted rocks, then sighed. She picked her wedgie over and over, then sighed. When we reached Nana's house, she went quiet. Her arms were as stiff as a couple of planks, flush against her body. Shit, are you my friend? she asked. Of course, you're the bestest friend I have, I said. No, I mean it. Are you my friend for real? Uh, yeah, I'm your friend for real. We watched a pair of ginger cats scamper down the road. She sighed again, then picked her wedgie. D'you think my ma was pretty? she asked out of the blue. Yeah, your ma was super-pretty. She looks super-super-pretty in that picture on your nightstand. Yeah, her hair was straight as a pin, even straighter'n mine, Isora said. Then she turned and walked away. I watched her zigzag down the hill with a limp from scratching her butt every few steps. She turned at the crossroads, all slow, slow like an old man with a cane and a Los Dos Caminos hardware store hat. Shit, won't you walk me to Melva's? Go on, y'know I always walk you.

Edwin Rivera

Boys grossed me out, but I thought I was supposed to fall in love with them. One time, before falling asleep, as the owls hooted on the other side of the window – I was sure owls were forest witches that had magicked into birds – my dad told me to think about nice things, because if I thought about things that were nice and things that I wanted to happen, I'd be able to fall asleep. I remember I started thinking about a boy from school who I thought I wanted to be my boyfriend. I pictured us walking up the road holding hands on a day with a white-hot sun, and it worked, I fell right asleep. After that, I did it every night and it worked every time. Even though it was the only thing that helped me sleep, the truth was that boys grossed me out big time, they grossed me out the same as the stink from the garbage trucks that drove up from the church while we played outside, as the white maggoty worms that squirmed out of the trash bins and out of dog buttholes and cat buttholes, and Nana said that if I kept pigging out on La Candelaria chocolate I'd have white maggoty worms too. Boys grossed me out the same as the juice that tinkled out of garbage bags, or like when Ma picked the cruddy bits out of her belly button and sniffed them because she thought nobody was looking, and it smelled like a road-killed rat stored in a shoebox for four years. When I grew up, I thought I wanted a boyfriend like Jerry Rivera, who was built like a fridgerator and had a fresh, clean-shaven face and hair slicked back with water. Or like Edwin Rivera, who was just as handsome, or maybe a little less than his brother. But only when I grew up. As a lilgirl I wanted nothing to do with boys.

That day, to get to the minimarket, we took the dirt path that cut through La Güerta School Footy Club. Ayoze and Mencey were on the pitch cannoning a ball between the goal posts. The goal posts were made of four hunks of rock, two on each side. Isora walked across the middle of the pitch and the boys started yelling at her. I didn't want to walk across the middle because I was scared they'd blooter the ball at me, but since Isora had done it I followed her like it was nothing. It all happened real fast. By the time I got to the other side, Isora'd already told the boys that sure, we'd stay and play with 'em. I didn't want to play with

Ayoze and Mencey because they grossed me out, just like all the other boys in the world except for Juanita Banana. They were crass and only ever wanted to play butt-tag, but Isora was crass too and maybe that's why she wanted to hang out with the boys that day. Because she was tired of playing Barbies and judgies and house and models and lazybones, and instead wanted to shoot stuff at birds and blow things up in the sky. It all happened real fast, so fast I didn't even realize I was on the back of Mencey's bike and that Isora was on the back of Ayoze's. They took us to a place below the minimarket, far far behind Bar de Antonio. It was a gigantic potato field with big, tall ferns all the way in the back, a bit like a forest with no pine trees and only ferns. A forest for little people.

It was seven or so at night on a mid-August day. Around that time, the sun crept up the side of El Amparo and finally peeked out from behind the grey clouds. We dropped the bikes at the property entrance and tore like goats through the tater field, which was as big as a football pitch, running and running, and as we bounded like goats we picked sourgrass and stuffed it in our mouths. Isora sucked on the sourgrass and so did Ayoze and Mencey, but I chewed it until the roof of my mouth tingled and a shiver went all through my body, and then we ran faster and faster, leaping over the tater plants and clambering on the rocks like goats. And as Nana said, goats were always looking for trouble.

After making a mess of the tater furrows, we came to a sudden stop at the end of the field and slammed right into the boys, who said whoa, awesome, when they saw how big and tall the ferns were. Then they got down on all fours and crawled through the grass. They went on and on until they were gobbled up by the forest of ferns and we couldn't see them any more. I looked at Isora and swallowed hard. My saliva was dry from the sourgrass, and the inside of my mouth was scratchy. Isora got down on all fours and started heading into the forest of ferns. C'mon, Shit! she said. But Iso, if I get home late they'll get cross with me, and she said, c'mon Shit, don't be lame. I looked up at the sky and saw that the sun was shining bright on the mountain of El Amparo. Sunlight grazed my shoulders, and I knew that when the sun was bright like that it meant the day was about to end. But I got down on all fours and went after Isora. I went after her because the thought of leaving her, of not seeing her until the next day, made me nervous. The forest of ferns swallowed us. First Isora, then me.

We heard the boys laughing and hollering up ahead but couldn't find them. We crept forward like two goat kids chasing after their goat mamas, and I could feel the rocks jabbing my knees and the ferns poking my head, and sometimes the ferns got so tangled up in my hair that I screamed. Right in front of me was Isora's ass in a pair of cut-off sweatshorts that were tied at the waist extra-tight. Through the shorts I could see her tatty red-and-white flower panties. Her ass was big and I liked watching it move, her whole kit on display, as my ma said, tudum tudum right and left. She moved so fast and so good you'd think she'd been crawling through that forest of ferns her whole life.

At the end of the tunnel was a plot of land that was practically empty, with a couple of fig trees and a mountain of debris. The boys were throwing rocks at the figs and watching them splat on the ground, laughing the whole time. Isora was breathing heavily. Mencey took a run-up and then sprinted on to the mountain of debris and Isora went after him. She didn't say that she was going or even look at me. My blood boiled. Forget about those jerks, said Ayoze. Lemme show you this super-awesome place behind the figs. I didn't want to go with him. I didn't want to be there. I didn't want to see the sun go down and down until it touched the tip-top of El Amparo. It was getting late and all I wanted was to grab Isora by the hair and kill her. I wanted to grab her by the ponytail and drag her along the floor behind me. I wanted to squeeze her. I wanted to squeeze her like a skink, like when kittens are tiny and I love them to bits but they won't give me the time of day and all I want to is to smoosh them until their eyes pop out of their heads.

I could hear Isora and Mencey laughing and hollering in the distance. I went with Ayoze, even though I didn't want to, kind of like when you get up to pee in the dead of night and creep down the hall like a ghost. We got to this huge rock wall with a big, dark hole in it. Ayoze said we should go in because it was super-awesome and a bit cooler. The hole in the cliffside was cave-like, with lots of pine needles scattered on the floor. It smelled of goats and of cat poop and like the stink in between the pads of a dog's paws. Get down on the floor, said Ayoze. For what, I asked. Because, he said. I got down on the floor and he got down on top of me, and the weight of his body felt like a cold slab of concrete on my chest and the little jaggedy rocks on the ground jabbed me in the back. His mouth smelled like raw egg, like the eggs spattered in chicken cack that I fetched from the chicken coop for Nana to fry, and she always had me pick out the eggs I wanted to eat, and I touched them one by one while singing *tin marín de dos pingüé, cúcara mátara títere fue*, and the egg I landed on was the one she fried for me.

A warm gust of cat poop blew in from the vulcano and swept across the cave floor. I wriggled a little because the rottedness was making me sick to my stomach, like when you get hit with a ball right in the middle, but the boy tightened his hold and did something with his hands. The wind whistled. I've gotta go, or else my ma'll get cross with me. Jus a bit longer. Pull down your jeans so we can try somethin'. Please, Ayoze, I mean it. My ma's gonna get pissed off. Jus another sec, he said. I shimmied down my jeans and he dragged my panties to my thighs and then I thought of a dream I had where Isora gave me a bathtub full of cats, and instead of bathing in water I bathed in cat fur and never got fur on my clothes ever again, and right then I felt a soft squidgy thing go up my minky and I thought I'd got a stomach cramp. It was a stabbing kind of pain, like when my dad ate a whole bag of loquats and a queso blanco sarnie and got so sick it came out of both ends, and my ma said you're not meant to mix loquats and dairy, specially if you're plannin' to hit the sack soon's you're done because the two things will go sour in your belly, and Ayoze was huffing like a dog with its tongue hanging out from being in the white-hot sun all day, a panting dog, my dad called it. Toby, cabrón! we heard a man yell, and Ayoze yanked his jeans back on with his chest pressed against mine. The scent of raw egg wormed up my nose like when you smell something you know you'll never forget, no matter how much time passes, and I took the fear that was eating away at me and used it to pull my jeans and panties back on. Ayoze's clothes were covered in dirt. I could see the tiny hairs starting to grow on his legs like thumb tacks. I got up and began picking the burrs and black-jacks off my shirt. Tooooooooby, we heard the man yell again. Isora and Mencey scrambled down the side of the debris and wound up right next to us. Iso, I'm leaving, I said. Iso, I'm leaving, and that was it, I walked out of there along the side of the field instead of crawling through the forest of ferns. When I got to the tater furrows, the sun was already squatting behind El Amparo. The clouds had made way for the light and everything then – the pines, the tater plants, the earth and the ocean that always showed me where the world ended – was orange.

Half a Kilo Off Each Tater

The day after the forest of ferns, I didn't visit Isora. I had fleas and ticks all over my minky and thighs and my whole body itched. All morning long Nana plucked them out, and every five seconds she asked me where the hell I'd been, chasing after raggedy, flea-ridden mutts I bet, I don't know where else you coulda gone and picked up all these fleas. The sound of the fleas popping beneath Nana's scratchy nails, while Nana hacked up a lung and said this phlegm'll be the end of me, I'm wrecked, miniña, made me want to burst into tears, like the time I fell in a bed of roses and geraniums and got all scratched up and all I could do was cry. Nana became upset from seeing me cry and cry for no reason but the ticks and fleas all over my minky and legs, and she said miniña, you've gotta go and get yourself blessed because, and I couldn't tell you why, but I reckon you've got susto, you're white as a sheet. And I knew, I knew all the way deep down in my heart that the ticks and the fleas and the susto had come from inside the cave, from when Isora left me all alone so she that could go off with that nasty gross boy.

The day after the forest of ferns, I didn't want to see Isora. The sound of her name made poison gurgle all the way up to the pit of my stomach. All morning I watched Nana putter, as she called it. We had milk and a buttered roll for breakfast. The bread came from the baker and had fennel seeds on it. I didn't like fennel seeds, so Nana picked them out for me with her fingers. We fed the hens and peeled taters in front of the TV. Nana got worked up seeing me peel the taters. She said I shaved half a kilo off each one. But I went on peeling, eyes glued to *Walker, Texas Ranger*, Nana's favourite television show. Tío Ovi came out of his room round lunchtime, and we ate taters with fried chicken and mojo. I thought of the way Isora ate Nana's chicken, the way she opened and closed her mouth like a dis- eased dog, like a dog that's been lost in the forest for weeks with nothing to eat and wolfs down rotted scraps of food from the trash bins without chewing. Isora chewed super-loud, her teeth were like feet squelching in the moss at the bottom of an empty pond.

When we finished lunch, Tío Ovidio went back to his room, where he watched Cantinflas movies, which were his favourite thing to watch besides telenovelas and *Corazón, Corazón*. The telenovela was playing on TV and I got itchy again from the bites on my thighs and minky. I screwed my hands into fists. My eyelids twitched from trying not to scratch myself. The image of Isora scrambling up the mound of debris with Mencey snuck into my head. I thought of when baby pigeons are weak and useless and fall from their nests because their bigger, better-fed siblings push them out and they go splat on the floor. That's what I was, a featherless chickling ridden with fleas, a chickling whose heart was tired and whose beak was open, waiting for Isora and for Isora's words, for the burnt-toast smell of her hair ends, for the black, cruddy undersides of her nails, which were like the sea at low tide pulling against the side of the bluff. I wanted to cry, I wanted Nana to cuddle me in her lap like a lilbaby, and I wanted the three days that I'd decided to give Isora the silent treatment for to be over, because I was starting to miss her. Whenever I was mad at Isora I liked to picture myself as a poor, unfortunate creature. I'd dream of breaking a leg or burning an arm on the cooker, just so she'd realize how much I mattered to her. But instead of breaking or burning myself, I just scratched at my panties until my bites were fiery like a vulcano. I didn't cry. I dug in my heels and carried on watching TV. From the kitchen, I could hear Tío Ovidio's watery laughter, his drowned-fish chuckle. Tío Ovidio who was always sad, Tío Ovidio who was always hunched over, who only ever laughed when the telenovela was on or when he watched Cantinflas movies.

That's when the phone rang, and I rushed to answer it. It was her. I felt the sound of her breath on the line like a stabbing pain. When she spoke, she sounded like someone who'd been eating gummy bears in secret, like a hamster with lots and lots of pumpkin seeds in its mouth. Hey, wanna play at the canal tomorrow? she asked. And even though I'd told myself I would hate her, I said yes, and I'd have said yes even if she'd walked on my back with heels on, even if she'd spat in my eyes, even if. I hung up. I heard Tío Ovidio's laughter in the background as I walked to the kitchen. I looked out the window and wondered why Tío Ovi had been shut away for so many years, why he'd been sick for so many years. Sick in the head, Ma said. Sick from all his manias, from being a maniac, Grandpa had said a gazillion years ago when I was a lilgirl and he still hadn't gone away. I looked out at the ocean, at the same dense, grey mass as always. And I thought the clouds were what made folks in the neighbourhood sad. The clouds fixed to the napes of all their necks. Right at the very tops of their spines. Right when the telenovela came on.

A Knife in the Chest

That morning the sky was so overcast that the whole neighbourhood was itching for it to rain or shine, so long as it made up its mind one way or the other. There were times when we wanted rain the way a person in agony wants a knife in the chest, like when a cat bites the limbs off a verdino lizard or tears the head off a skink and the poor creature carries on twitching like it's not actually dead, like it doesn't need a head to survive. We were convinced the sky was messing around with us, just like a cat toying with its prey. When Nana saw that the lizards and skinks were in pain, she'd smash them with a rock and squish them on the floor. Poor little guys, I'd whisper as they died, but then Nana'd explain that they were hurting and what they needed was for somebody to kill them.

Time had passed and I'd stored the memory of the forest of ferns in a small room in my head. Me and

Isora were friends like always, but there was something inside me, under my eyes and in my ears, that stopped me from being happy, heart and soul. Everything Isora did bothered me. I'd always loved the way she moved, the stuff she said, the plastic squeak of her sneakers on the tarmac, the dry snap of her panties against her butt cheek when she picked a wedgie. But not any more. Those days everything Isora did rubbed me the wrong way. Every time she ripped a fart, I hated her. Every time she said c'mon, Shit, don't be lame, I wanted to bite off her head. Every time she went up the hill too fast and left me eating dust, I had the urge to grab her by the ponytail and drag her on the ground from the start of the road all the way to the pine trees at the very top. I still loved her. At the same time I hated her, I hated her so much that in the end, well.

The sky was leaden that day and Isora didn't call on the phone. She showed up at Nana's out of the blue and threw a pebble at the kitchen window. Nana startled in her chair and put her hand on her chest, like something bad was about to happen. Sus, muchacha, what's that clatter? she asked and stared at the window. I think it's Isora, I answered. I reached over the bucket of water on the counter and there she was standing under the dark sky, which cast shadows all over her body, making her look ancient, like she was a million years old. Even though I didn't want to hang out, I tapped the window twice and went outside. She said let's go to the computer room and chat on mésinye with the kids from school.

For a few minutes we pretended to pay attention to the computer teacher, who'd already forgiven us for the incident with carlossion's huge willy. Then Isora carefully opened mésinye and started saying hi to everybody in school with an account, which was like four or five kids tops. After a while of hey sup? what u up 2? im bored & u? im alrite, Isora logged on to the Terra chat room without asking. All the anger I'd stored up came pouring out. What're you doing, Iso? You promised we wouldn't, I said, trying to keep my voice down. Don't be a dumbass, Shit, I'll jus be a sec, she responded. Then I'm leaving, I said back. Don't be a dumbass, she repeated. And I yelled, don't *you* be a dumbass! The computer teacher walked up to us and stood there with his arms crossed over his chest, staring us dead in the eyes, the huge sweat stains on his shirt reeking of dead dog, and then he said that that was it, he wouldn't be letting us back in ever again, he was a peaceful guy who didn't like trouble and all we ever did was distract the other students, cause problems and not pay attention. I got up in a rage and flew out of the room. Isora joined me a few seconds later, and when I saw the smug smile on her face, that dumbass smile that smoothed her chin dimple and her chin mole and the tiny hair that stuck out of her chin mole, I shoved her against the wall, I shoved her as hard as I could. And she said what d'you think you're doing? Have you lost it, or what? then shoved me back. I grabbed a handful of her skin and twisted it until she started howling like an animal on its deathbed. Then she pulled me by the hair and shook me. All the kinkis came out to watch and started yelling get her! crack her head! smash her on the floor! kick her in the back! My blood boiled so hot that I took Isora by the shoulder and sank my teeth into her neck. The kinkis were still hooting. That's when I realized that Isora's anger was like a tidal wave. In that moment, right in that moment, I knew that I didn't want to hurt her, that I wanted us to stop no matter what. But it all happened so fast, and I don't know if I had the chance to tell her. Isora dragged her big, heavy fist from the side of her body all the way to my face. Her fist hovered in the air for less than a second, just long enough for the shape of her dark, balled-up fingers to be seared in my memory. Then she brought down her fist. She brought it down like I was a pig and my face was its snout, like when they stun the pig before slaughtering it. I stayed right where I fell. I stared up at the clouds, which were like blocks of lead. Big and slow and so grey they were almost silver. Someone yelled holy shit, she's been KO'd! I saw my blood drip on to my thighs. It was shiny, like melted red-glitter marbles or my like Ma's old nail polish. My mouth tasted of Tío Ovi's tin cup, my mouth tasted of Isora when we kissed behind the cultural centre.

Back When Isora Didn't Exist

I'd been playing on the Gameboi for two days straight. Ever since me and Isora fought outside computer class, I'd said almost nothing for two whole days. I had an awful pain in my mouth from where I'd been whacked and another pain in my neck from holding my body extra-stiff while I played Pokémon to keep from thinking. The truth is, I was no good at Pokémon. Isora usually helped me. When she wasn't around, I always wound up battling hundreds and hundreds of Ratikats from inside the weeds with a Squirtle that Isora had nicknamed BIRDBRAIN. Nana had been on my case all day, saying I should go outside and catch some sun, that I was whiter than a silent-but-deadly, that I couldn't stay curled up like that all the time, but I just carried on wham-bamming the Rati-kats and popping in and out of Pokémon stadiums and reading and rereading the same old conversations with the same old dum-dums on the same old screen with my mouth in pain and my lips swollen like a woman who'd just had them injected, all so I wouldn't have to think about what'd gone on between Isora and me.

On day three I took out my Gameboi and set it on the kitchen table. Nana was picking the fennel seeds off the bread, and she turned to me and said miniña, won't you go'n fetch us a smidge of cheese, ham and a smidge of bread? I'm too wrecked to head down there on these busted old legs. My first thought was that the last thing I wanted to do was go to the minimarket and see Isora, that my face still hurt from when she'd whacked me, that my heart was in tatters and would be almost impossible to mend, that just thinking about the kinkis and about Isora's face – as if Isora'd murdered me with a gunshot somewhere up in a drizzly forest – got my guts all in a knot. Then again, maybe it'd be a good thing if Isora saw me at the market looking super-chill about the fact that she wasn't my friend and I wasn't hers, maybe that way she'd know, maybe that way she'd understand that I wasn't planning on forgiving her, that seeing her there had zero effect on me, that I could go to the market for a smidge of bread and cold meats while she stood there watching me like a duck in a ponytail as I walked right through the door and into the market.

I headed down the road with Nana's order for threehundredfifty grams of ham and twohoundredfifty grams of cheese knocking around my head. The calima was thick, as it always was in late August. The sky was covered in the same tired, grey strip of low clouds. The moment Nana told me how much cold meat and cheese to get, the very second she gave me the order, I'd start listing the amounts in my head, over and over, just to make sure I wouldn't forget. Half the time it slipped my mind because as soon as I got to the minimarket, me and Isora'd start chatting, which meant I'd stop listing the amounts in my head. Then I'd have to call Nana on Chela's phone and ask her to remind me what she wanted and how much. But that day was going to be different, that day I knew for sure I wouldn't forget because I wanted to show Isora that I could give less of a damn about talking to her.

Sinson was scooting his butt on the ground outside the market, like he had an itchy something in his guts and wanted the tarmac to scratch him all over, inside and out. I laughed quietly. Me and Isora loved it when Sinson did that and always hollered at him yeah, scritch your butthole, Sinson, scritch it! But this time I kept the thought to myself, because I wanted to look serious as I entered the minimarket. Chela was checking out a wino that everyone called Ramoncín who'd bought five boxes of wine and put them on the counter all in a row, like he was playing with dolls. She was adding the wine to a tab that took up a whole page and belonged to Ramoncín's wife, who'd been dressing in black every day since her dad died and was constantly whining about what a hard time her husband gave her, the poor thing. Chuchi was slicing cold meats with her head down as she listened to the customers yakking with her ma about other people. And there in the back, all the way in the back of the market, was Isora. I saw her and felt as if something had smacked me in the face. She had on cut-off sweatshorts and the same sweater she always wore, the one with the watermelon slices dotted with black seeds, the one that made her sweat like an old hog. It was her, except she looked like a whole different person. Someone several years older and much prettier and more serious. I wondered how someone could change so much in just three days. Oh, miniña, how's that mouth holdin' up? asked Eulalia, as she waited for Chuchi to finish slicing her cold meats. Ggggood, I answered, all quiet and sad, my voice wretched-sounding and quivery, and then glanced over at Isora, who was shelving cans of corn. Her expression stayed the same, she didn't even change her posture. She listened to my voice the way people listen to silence. Chuchi and Chela didn't look at me either, they didn't even tell me to rot in hell. I figured our fight had embarrassed them, because they were famous and lived in the more central part of the neighbourhood.

I went up to the deli counter and reeled off the order in a single breath, like I was throwing up, three-hundredfiftyofham, twohundredfiftyofcheese. Hunh? Chuchi said like she was so disgusted she could've choked. Chacha, this girl here is soft in the head and her mother doesn't even know it! said Chela as she continued to jot things down in the ledger. Give her four hundred of ham and three hundred of cheese. Chuchi put her head down and started slicing. The machine hummed against the nub of ham and I looked over at Isora. She still hadn't responded to the fact that I was there. I was dying for her to look at me so that I could look away and so she could see the hatred in my eyes, as well as the number she'd done on my mouth. But she didn't look at me, not even for a second. Then Melva, the one that lived above the market, came in, and she and Chela and Eulalia started having a chat. Lala, muchacha, remember Isabelita, the one from Redondo? Turns out her girl's got herself knocked up, Melva told Eulalia. Sus, muchacha, isn't that one still a teeny bit wet behind the ears? Eulalia answered. It's an epidemic, Melva went on. Which one's that, again? I forget, asked Eulalia. The youngest, muchacha, said Chela, the one that's always traipsing around with her tits on display. She's no older than fourteen, fifteen tops. Chuchi passed Chela the ham and cheese and I asked in a quiet voice if I could have a loaf of bread. She carried on with the other women as she fetched the bread for me. She didn't look at me even once. She put the loaf in a grocery bag, then thumbed through the ledger to the page with Nana's name on it. She ran her finger down the grid until she'd run out of paper and then she did it again, over and over, until she was on page four, which is where Nana's tab ended and where Chela wrote down how much we owed her this time, and then shut the ledger.

I walked out of the minimarket. I felt like some evil creature had got in my belly, a green, gnarly lizard that was kicking me on the inside. Sinson came out to bark at the man who delivered the baked goods. Shhht, shut your hole, Sinsoncabrón! Chela screamed from inside the market. I thought of how long Nana's tab was compared to other people's. I thought of how Ma paid off a couple of items every week because, like Dad said, they were riding the dollar now and laughing all the way to the bank. But Nana's list was super-long, about as long as two Isoras standing on top of each other, and I understood then that not even boatloads of money, not even shiploads of money, as Dad said, not even the holiday homes and the hotels and the construction could save Nana from the debt Grandpa had buried them in before he packed up and left. Next thing I knew, I was at Nana's cousin's house. The one with two women living under the same roof. There was his wife, the clever one, and her sister, who kept the house spick and span and looked after the land too. And as I walked past, I saw his wife seated on a plastic chair, fanning herself with an HiperDino coupon magazine. She had on a floral dress, a blue sunhat and red kitten heels. Her eyes were all made up, and so were her lips and nails. Her sister was out weeding the field, hunched over like a fig tree bent under the wind. Her face was like the charred bark on a pine tree, leathery and dark. It was the same as Nana's and Doña Carmen's, and it was the same as Ma's. Like it'd come from another time, back when people lived in caves and slept on the ground with their dogs. When there was no tarmac, no cultural centre and no minimarket, no bar and no church, back when there were no cement mixers churning and no beamers hugging the road, when there were no Gamebois and no Babybjörns with wee-wee holes, no cell phones and no cell-phone cases, no mésinye. Back when Isora didn't exist and I didn't exist either, back when we weren't friends just like we weren't friends now.

the last thing left

a hole in the ground dug with nails and soil and the
blood of your nails in your ears to be buried maybe
it was best to be buried like the dead and to be an
underground thing to become the root of an ancient
plant to become something almost edible and be eaten
by accident by a lizard by a sick animal with tattered
insides and maggot-ridden on the outside rotted like
a rabbit with rabies and with no mother or father and
with a taste of banana plantation toxins on the roof
of your mouth maybe fosferno maybe the best thing
was to have boulders hanging above your head like
passion fruit sliced open with the molar tips to yank
your teeth out one by one with a pair of pliers and set
them all each and every one on a plate slathered in
mayo the lot of them piled up like loaded fries and
to feed on your own teeth like a dog eating its own
turd till you've gone full circle like a pair of socks till

you've disappeared till your own teeth eat your own self inside-first and you have your guts pulled out of your butthole like a goat with a detached uterus and to make a seashell necklace out of those guts and then think of giving the necklace to isora and then think of giving a teeny bit of bile juice to isora which is the last thing that's left when there's nothing left

Like Night Moths in the Sky

Nana headed to the fields in the early morning. She went out to feed the hens. She left bright-bright and early, as the rooster was still crowing, and while she was at it she picked some tagasastes for the rabbits too. When she came home, I heard her make a right clatter as she walked in the door. Behind her was Juanita Banana, dragging a beat-up skateboard his dad got for buying a set of armchairs for the TV room. It'd been a few days since me and Isora stopped talking, a few days that'd soon become a week. It was the longest I'd ever gone without speaking with her. Before we knew it, school would be starting up again. Before we knew it, the fiesta committee would be up on their extra-long ladders that were tall as pine trees stringing little pieces of paper between the lamp posts. Just like that, zigzagging up the neighbourhood, all lined up in a row like ballerinas. Let's skate downhill without brakes on! Juanita said as he hopped about, body folded in the middle. I don't feel like it, I answered, and stayed right where I was in the armchair, curled up like a centipede. C'mon chacha, y'know we always have a good time, he said, and pulled me off the cushions by the arms. Let go, Juanito! I cried. Pffft, I'm just tryina save you from dying of boredom. I said no, chacho! I cried again, and turned to face the TV. C'mon, chacha, please, he whispered. Piss off, Juanita Banana, you dumb fuck, I said in a voice that was unlike my own, a strange voice that'd never come out of my mouth before. He froze, blinking back tears. Nana stepped out of the kitchen with the coffee pot, alarmed by what she'd heard. The sound of my own voice had alarmed me too. I curled up in the armchair again and listened to Juanita leave, I listened to him walk out the door with his skateboard behind him like a bagful of junk dragged across the floor.

I was super-quiet that day, just like I'd been all the other days since I'd stopped being Isora's friend. The whole time, I had this Aventura song stuck in my head. The song was about love and pride and rejection and it went *adónde irá este amor? Todita la ilusión? Me pregunto a cada instante, yo sé que yo fallé pero tu orgullo y tu actitud me impiden recuperarte, niegas sentir amor, ocultas la pasión y también me rechazas, conmigo no podrás, te conozco de más, tú todavía me amas.* Nana kept coming to the TV room loaded with meringues and sugar donuts and guava paste and goat's cheese sarnies and Libby's juice, but I wanted none of it. Sus, miniña, she said, you'd best ask your ma to get you blessed 'cause, from where I'm standin', it looks to me like you've got susto, and then she put her hand on my head like I had a fever. What I had was Isora fever, I thought. At six or so in the evening, as I twisted and turned in the armchair because my back hurt like crazy from being curled up there all day, Nana said get your shoes on, miniña, let's take a walk up Donkey's Pass at th'very least. I buried my head in a cushion and shut my eyes. Nana put on my sneakers and did up my laces and then pulled me out of the armchair by the shoulders. We went outside. My eyes stung in the light and the clouds were so pale and bright that they made the whole world look washed out. I walked behind Nana, my eyes open no more than a sliver, like a small sleepwalking child. Everything seemed fake – the fig tree leaves, the cactus spines, the few clumps of sourgrass that still sprung up here and there, the numbers on the houses. We went up Donkey's Pass till we were right outside Ofelia's, an old ginger-haired lady with a beautiful jungly garden who always invited Nana over for coffee after the tele-novela. I didn't want to see the old bag, so I made like I was headed towards the holiday homes, but

Nana went straight to Ofelia's front door and said not
so fast, miniña, we'll be havin' none of that. None
of you walkin' up there on your own. Ofeeeeé, she
yelled from the back entrance. Is that you, Almeríín?
C'mon in, said Ofelia, I've got a pot of coffee on the
boil. Nana went in and told me to sit outside with the
kitty-cats, nice and quiet. I went down the path of
glittered stones that Ofelia'd laid in her garden and
sat on the edge of a bed of yellow flowers next to the
front steps. Ofelia's garden was so lush it looked like a
small forest. There were sea daffodils growing in every
corner, and hydrangeas and hibiscus flowers the size
of my head. There were geraniums in all the colours
of the rainbow, as well as calla lilies, echium, pansies
and yellow roses that looked like they'd come straight
out of one of Ma's home décor magazines. I sat there
for a while and stared into the middle distance as
I thought of the time Isora told me that the reason
Ofelia's husband left her was because she refused to
do the nasty with him at night, because it made her
tired. And I thought that maybe Ofelia put all the
energy she didn't have for doing the nasty into making the garden so pretty it was almost a jungle.

All of a sudden, I felt Ofelia's beautiful flowers
had given me strength, so I jumped to my feet and
headed up Donkey's Pass towards the holiday homes,
all alone on my own. I picked a vinagrera leaf and

nibbled on it. The vulcano was quilted in clouds, and a low fog wavered between the sheets that'd been set out to dry on the rooftops of the house. Donkey's Pass wasn't paved, and even though the people that lived there had laid down cement, Nana said it wasn't long ago that the road had been pure dirt. As I headed up to the holiday homes, I munched absently on the vinagrera. That whole week I'd felt like there'd been somebody inside me calling the shots. I reached the front gate of the holiday homes and clambered on to a bed of small pine trees that was off to the side. I sat on the tall part of the wall, next to where my ma went in when she couldn't find her keys. The tourists were in the pool, they were splashing about and sunbathing in the sunless weather and eating sausages, the spicy kind, at terrace tables under palm-leaf umbrellas. I thought they must be having dinner because Ma said that the disgusting tourists always had an early dinner, at six o'clock. All I could see from high up on the wall were old people, old people roasting in the sun like big, dark crabs. I sat there for a while, watching the tourists slather on sunscream, eat grilled sausages with ketchup and dice tomatoes into small cubes for the salad, like perfect little dolls in a perfect little dollhouse. A girl about my age ran past, she was white-blonde, pale and long-limbed, almost see-through. I stared at her for a long time like a cat that stares at a fly smashing into a kitchen window. She had blue eyes and yellow, gappy teeth as big as shovels. She looked foren, and I sat up on the wall and said to her helou, yu lai tu plei? And she laughed and laughed with her rotted teeth, with her stinky rat teeth. No lai? I asked again. She smiled and said I don't speak English, I'm from Madrid. The words whistled out the gaps between her teeth. She spoke like they did on TV, like they did in cartoons – just as fancy, just as schmancy-pantsy as they did. Let's go play in the woods, I know this super-awesome place I can show you, I said. She thought about it for a second, her mouth hanging open, her hands behind her back and a dumb look on her face. Okay, give me a sec, and she sprinted over to an old man who I guessed was her grandad.

My legs shook as I waited anxiously outside the door to the summer house. I didn't think of Isora as I waited. Or I did. I thought of how I wouldn't die from not being her friend, of how there were other girls in the sea. That's when the Madrid girl showed up in a dress with blue flowers that matched her eyes, and a yellow Loro Parque hat (and I used to think Loro Parque hats were for dum-dums) and the kind of hiking boots that foreners were always wearing. The girl followed me without a question. She hummed songs I didn't know, and each step she took was more fearful than the last, as if the ground might cave in beneath her, into the centre of the island. Is your school really far away? she asked in her squeaky-rat voice. I take the guagua, I said. Hahaha, a guagua's a bus, isn't it? Uh, a guagua's a guagua, I said, a bit miffed. Haha, she laughed with her stuck-out teeth resting on her bottom lip, and then she held my hand.

I'd never had a friend to hold hands with before. Hers made mine itch. We walked past the pen with the goats that belonged to the man who sold Nana goat's cheese. We walked past the stables of the horses that belonged to the Horse family, past a raised bed with berries in it that belonged to a couple of tourists that Nana called the Lushes, and I never got why they planted berries when there were brambles on the side of the road, and then we reached the topmost houses on Donkey's Pass, the houses that looked out on to the forest. And without thinking or talking about it we headed into the pine trees, all the way to a place I'd never been to before, past the places Isora had shown me, because it was Isora who showed me that place and every other place I knew.

We sat on a couple of low rocks with ferns all around, and our hands never let go even though they were getting sweaty. The forest was dark and thickety and the mist was at the level of our heads. As we sat there like that we looked like night moths in the sky, a sky of pine needles and low-lying clouds. What do you usually play? she asked out of the blue, squeezing my hand. I shrugged, uhhh whatever, like dolls. She picked up a pine cone and made it move like a person. Everyone in the Canary Islands is so nice, haha, she said and stuck out her teeth. I gave her a half-forced smile and thought this chick's a bit thick isn't she. I let go of her hand and scratched at the bark on a pine tree. Did you know witches live in this forest, and that they can turn themselves into black hunting dogs? You're lying, haha! she said. Am not, everyone in the neighbourhood knows it, sometimes the witches leave huge gross turds in the patios of the houses. Is that true? she said, already scared. Yeah, and I can talk to 'em too. How? They leave me notes in the barks of the pine trees. Really? Yeah, and if you don't do what they say they come to your room in the middle of the night and take you. And then what? They bring you to the woods. Really? Yeah, and that tree over there, it's got something written on it. What does it say? It says bite my minky or I'll kill you. What's a minky? A minky's a minky. I pulled down my jeans but left my panties on. They were purple with white lace and a cat on them with the words meow-meow in English. The mainland girl took her rat-teeth, her little miniony rat-teeth, and bit on my minky. She bit me fast, like when you do something you don't want to. I looked down at her. Seeing her made me think of Isora, of how there was no other girl in the world like her. I remembered the way Isora's eyes got when she cried – swampy and green like a frog in a pond. By the time the girl got up from the ground there was fog all around us and up there, way up above the pine trees, way up above our heads, I could see the peak of the vulcano.

Grinding on My Own

I saw Isora all over the place. I saw her hanging on the wall like a tiny little virgin carved in hardwood. Like the Virgen de Candelaria I saw her, naked and hovering, like a virgin without her cloak, which is just a stick with a long, pinched head. I'd hallucinate about her before bed – a ghost shuffling through every room, howling sad Aventura songs at three in the morning. I had Isora on a small TV screen that played in front of my face non-stop. I pictured her grinding on doorframes. I watched *Walker, Texas Ranger* and turned round every few minutes to see if she was behind me, grinding her minky on the arm-chair cushions. I heard noises and felt scared. Isora was a dog hidden in a locked room, I felt her panting inside my head, I felt her wet snout touch my spine and make the peach fuzz on my back stand on end. And I grinded, I grinded alone for the first time, without Isora, though I imagined she was beside me. Isora touching herself with a crayon from school as she watched *La mujer en el espejo*. Isora touching herself after they cancelled *Pasión de Gavilanes* because of the thing that happened with the Twin Towers, which they showed over and over on the news. Isora when she said Shit, give this pen a try, it's longer and fatter. Isora when she shoved a clothes peg all the way up her minky. Isora. Isora was no longer my friend. Me when I grinded on my own without Isora. Me when I grinded and cried at the same time. Me when I grinded until I bled. The stink of genitals and rust. Rust-covered genitals. All day I grinded on my own, until the whole house shook, until rocks tumbled down the crags, until the pine trees and tabaibas turned to face the other way, until the tabaibas and the loquats and the donkeys leaked milk. I grinded until I saw the vulcano stir. Then the municipal alarm blared and they interrupted *El Chavo del 8* so that the mayor could get on TV and say quiet down, everyone, quiet down, while small white letters below him read GET YOUR THINGS AND JUMP IN THE SEA, MISNIÑOS, SAVE YOURSELVES WHILE YOU CAN. And then Nana and Tío Ovi and Mami and Papi gathered their belongings and loaded them into wheelbarrows and pushed them into a huge truck, and I shoved Nana's cats into tater sacks

and hauled them into the truck too, and then I stuffed
Tío Ovi's canary into a pocket of my jeans and we
drove down to Chela's minimarket, and because of the
fear that the disaster had stirred up, the fear that the
vulcano would kill every last one of us, Isora became
my friend again, and we said GET IN, WE'LL
TAKE YOU TO LA GOMERA, BECAUSE
NO ONE IS SAFE FROM THE VULCANO.
And Chela, Chuchi and Isora climbed in the truck.
Isora had on a dress that her ma had worn to a chris-
tening one time. And they piled all the food from the
minimarket into the back of the truck. All the boxes
of liquorice and packets of tater chips with Tazos
inside them and all the gummy bears and the boxes of
Camel Balls bubble gum and all the canned beef we
needed to make spaghetti with meat sauce when we
got to La Gomera. And a cute red pricing gun in case
we had to make some dough by selling the minimarket's wares on the sandy beach. From the distance
we could see the lava, which was almost at the church.
It had gobbled up the topmost houses and oozed over
our house too, and now my home sweet home was
just a mountain of debris, a mountain of debris and
charred cat poop. I saw my bed afloat on the lava like
a boat at sea. By then the truck was floating on the
ocean, and all around it were planks of wood and
banana leaves that had flapped through the air when

the vulcano erupted. We watched the lava devour the neighbourhood and the island, and then Isora held my hand and suddenly we were the kinds of friends who loved each other and said I love you. And my ma was done with the hotels and the holiday homes, and my dad was done working in construction. Me and Isora turned back, and we looked over the tater sacks full of cats and over the packets of Munchitos potato chips and over the kilos and kilos of canned beef, and saw the land turned into pure fire. The lava from the vulcano blanketed everything. We saw the island sink into the ocean and the ocean devour the island, then burp up a bubble of air, and everything went dead quiet, as though there was never anything there to begin with – no island, no neighbourhood, not even a girl in that neighbourhood grinding alone until she bled, until she stank of genitals and rusted nails.

Creepy-crawly Lizard

I set out to find Isora at the first glow of day. I walked down the road real slow, slower than slow, like when you fumble through a room with the lights off. I walked down the road with Isora on my mind, with what I'd say to her when I saw her on my mind. I thought of how I couldn't go another week without being her friend, that I didn't care how small I had to make myself, or if I wound up having to behave like a creepy-crawly lizard. I was a creepy-crawly lizard, I thought. And I didn't mind it at all. I scanned for her down there, down at the end of the road, where the sky and the sea merged into one. I pictured her squinched over like a hunting dog as she wolfed down Sinson's dog food in one gulp, there on a corner of the road. Eyes bulging, the stink of garbage in her teeth, dirt tears tracking down her grimy face. I'm so sorry, Shit, please forgive me, I imagined her saying.

The minimarket was closed when I got there. Sinson was chewing on the tip of his tail with the few busted teeth he had left. The back door to the house was open, as always. I tiptoed down the hall and found her in front of the bathroom mirror, putting her hair up in a ponytail like she did every day. Isora always wore her hair slicked back against her skull with water. She'd wet the brush and tense her scalp, then pull her hair into a super-duper-tight ponytail with a few loose curls. Her hairline started too close to her eyes. She looked like a girl from the Guanche period, before the conquest. She had dark-dark skin and eyes like a pair of shiny green lights. She had a pinched head and a chin dimple that looked like it got bigger by the day. A chin dimple that was practically a woodpecker's nest, perfectly round, like it'd been pecked out with a beak.

Isora spotted me in the mirror. She said let's go to th'other side of Redondo, where the neighbourhood ends, I'm sick of seein' the same old fuckin' thing over'n over. She said it without turning round, she said it to my reflection in the filthy, fogged-up mirror that had lots of humidity stains eating away at the corners. She said it just like that, like she'd never punched me in the kisser. And I said okay, Iso, like she'd never thumped me in the kisser. She brushed her teeth. She didn't have a shirt on. She wore a white stretchy bra that Chela had bought for her at El 99 when she turned nine and got her first period, on the same day as her birthday. She spat out blood when she rinsed because she always brushed her teeth too hard. She only rinsed once, leaving her mouth and chest spattered with toothpaste. She turned on the tap and the water washed the pinkish mixture below ground. In my head I saw Isora's blood streaming down the pipes and through the island. She wiped her mouth on her arm and sponged up the menthol spiciness that was still on her stache. She sat on the toilet bowl and stared at me like a dog taking a dump in a field. She had on one of those panty liners that smelled of bin juice and had black smudges all over. It wasn't period blood, it was melted tarmac. I looked at her, and for a second I felt ashamed. She wiped herself and got up. I saw her freshly shaven minky all red and inflamed and blotchy with welts. I wanted to hug her, I wanted to feel the milk and gofio churning in her guts like a cement mixer at full tilt. As usual, I did nothing. I waited for her to finish getting dressed and then we left.

We took the trail by the canal. Isora walked in front, parting the thicket of plants with her hands and whipping the branches of heather at me. I walked behind with my eyes fixed on her ponytail. It never worried me that I didn't know how to get home on my own. Isora was my guide through El Drago Park and I was her disgusting tourist. It was like when I couldn't tell the time and Isora checked her winnydapoo watch and said it's twelve fifteen and I believed what she said was true, that it was twelve fifteen, which meant I didn't have to try and teach myself things she was already good at, like reading the kitchen clock or adding and subtracting with your fingers or peeling apples or counting money or figuring out how many gummy bears you could buy with a euro or whether to pull up your panties when a boy in a cave takes them off or how to take the trail by the canal to where the neighbourhood ends.

We stepped over the broken slabs of concrete where we'd wet our feet. Isora stopped, pulled down her jeans and her panties and peed in the canal. A splash of blood and wee for the folks downstream, she said, and then shimmied herself dry over the running water. We carried on until we reached the point where the canal wasn't covered any more. We turned on to a dirt road. There was a pair of rough, white walls on either side and we ran our fingers along the bumps of paint. Further ahead, near the end of the road, was a green gate with the words BEWARE VISHUS DOG and next to it BEWARE POIZUN. Two monstrous dogs barked on the other side of the wall. Shut up you puto foquin mutt, Isora yelled as she hurled rocks over the gate. Stupid mutt, gross slobbery devil-dog! We stayed close to the wall on the opposite side of the road and hurried past, like when you have to pee in the dead of night after watching a scary movie. Isora grabbed my arm and said watch out, Shit, that's where Gloria the witch lives, the one that learned witchcraft in Cuba, and then she pointed at a small house with a broken window. How come you know a witch lives there? I asked her. My nan told me she brought my ma here one time to get blessed 'cause she had a susto that wasn't goin' away. Is she bad? I asked. No, she's not bad, she helps people with their problems, she answered. Then how come she didn't fix your ma? I asked. The hairs on my arms stood on end. Isora said nothing. We carried on. I walked right beside her and she held my arm extra hard, so hard that it hurt.

We got to a great big open lot. There were tyre marks from motorcycles and skid marks too. Right across the way, next to a plum tree, was a dirty old sign that read REDONDO. All of this used to belong to my grandpa José Casiano, she said, pointing at the lot. All of it? Yeah, Shit. Now they use it for racin' motorcycles and mopeds and stuff. La bitch says she never met 'im, that he was a fat, rich guy who smoked cigars in Venezuela. For real? Yeah, la bitch never met 'im 'cause he had a hundred eleven kids with more than forty women. He slept with a different woman every night. Holy cow! D'you mean it, chacha? I asked, a teensy bit suspicious because there were times when I didn't know if Isora was making stuff up and a hundred eleven children was a lot of children. Yeah, I guess he musta always been wantin' sex, or else he wouldna had so many kids. I guess his willy musta been all messed up. Yeah, I guess so, I said, even though I didn't totally understand how kids were made. Slow and careful, we reached the sign that said Redondo. We picked a couples of vinagrera leaves and started munching on them. Isora stopped. Shit, she said, and then looked me in the eye. What? I asked. I'm scared to keep going. Why? I said with a teensy bit of fear. I'm kinda scared of leavin' the neighbourhood, she said, and her hands shook a little. We sat on a big rock. I said nothing. I looked up at the clouds drifting across the sky. They were extra-dark and low down on our heads. I had the feeling the rain would start any second. To be honest, I'm kinda scared too, I told her later. That's what I said, but to be honest I wasn't scared. I wasn't even a teeny bit scared, to be honest.

By the time we turned back, the rain was pissing down on everything. We headed the way of the dogs that'd barked their heads off and saw Gloria unpegging the laundry from the clothes line outside her house. Isora raised her hand in the distance, gave her the finger, and said foc yu bruja bitch! Then she pulled me by the arm and legged it. We ran and ran until we were almost at the canal, and a man went by with a giant sack of tagasastes for the rabbits. Byeeeee, Mr Damián, said Isora as she ran. Sus, miniña, it's been so long since I seen ya I thought for sure it was yer ma I saw in the fog, he said from beneath the sack. Isora was breathing so fast I thought her heart would shoot right out of her chest. We ran past the lifted-up slabs. Kilos and kilos of pine needles crowded the water. We sprinted across the canal. The ground was slippery. I fell flat on my butt and got water all the way down my back, cutting up my elbows and hands. You'll be okay, Shit, said Isora, her face dripping wet. I got back on my feet and we carried on running. It was raining like the world was about to end. Down there, down in the big, dark sea, lightning split the clouds. We were behind the cultural centre and Isora took cover under a bit of roof. She said come here, Shit, let's wait for it to ease up. We sat on the floor. We were basically water, Isora and me, that's how wet we were. Shit, d'you wanna kiss like boyfren and girlfren? she asked out of the blue. Okay, I said, and shrugged. She closed her eyes and pressed her lips to mine. My eyes stayed open. Her face was so close that I couldn't see. I still hurt on the inside from the punch, and my lips were still swollen as well. I forced open my mouth and stuck out my tongue. Her eyelashes brushed my face. They were extra-long and spiny like needles. Her tongue was cold, pure ice. Her tongue was like the snow on a dormant vulcano.

Colourful Papers Fluttered Over the Square

The day after me and Isora made up, it was already September. I knew it was September because a rocket woke me. BAM it went when it blew up in the sky like a bomb. The dogs and the hens and the rabbits startled and then fussed in the fields. I could hear Pepe Benavente playing in the distance and the voice of the committee president blaring through the bull-horn as he said how nice the neighbourhood looked. I ate a small spoonful of powdered milk with sugar and dialled the only number I knew by memory with my heart hoppity-hopping in my chest. Chuchi answered, her voice thin as a thread. She's not in, miniña. She's gone to th'beach, to Teno, with her cousin from Santa Cruz. Should be back round eight this evenin' at the latest.

It wasn't even eleven in the morning when I went outside to wait. The road was crawling with committee members. Every last one of them was there, with their Dorada beer hats and their boulder-like bellies. The president had already climbed atop the lamp post and he was busy stringing up colourful pieces of paper. There was already paper zigzagged from the bottom of the neighbourhood all the way to the crossroads. Tiiiiiiiiito, muchacho, can't you see it's crooked? hollered the president at one of the men with the rockets. Leave it the fuck alone, I'm puttin' it straight, aren't I? Or maybe you're too dumb to notice. All you're ever good for is mouthin' off. And the rocket man went and sent another firework into the sky. The dogs were barking their heads off again. You could even hear the Horse family's horses whinnying like devils in their stables. I sat and waited. It wasn't even noon yet when I squatted outside Gracián's, the one with eyebrows like a pair of centipedes. I scooped a fistful of gravel from the street and let it slide through my fingers one piece at a time, as though each bit of gravel stood for an hour between now and the moment Isora would show up again, there, at the end of the road. The president climbed down his extra-tall ladder and hitched up his trousers, which hung loose around his waist and were belted with shoelaces. That's me done, he said. And if you don't like it, that's your problem. It looked to me like they weren't going to be stringing any colourful papers up our street, even though Nana'd hung out her Spanish flag and her Virgen del Rosario banner, which was blue with silver sparkles. I raised my voice a little – me, the one who was always too scared and embarrassed to talk to grown-ups – and said Tito, aren't you gonna string the papers higher up the street? No, miniña, this year we're only goin' far as the crossroads, that Tony Tun Tun milked us for all we're worth and we're flush out. If people from here on up want any paper decorations, they'll have to do it themselves. The president took the step ladder and closed it. Another song by Pepe Benavente, which wasn't really by Pepe Benavente but by another musician, mingled with the sound of dogs barking. The song was about betrayal and forgiveness, and it went *oye traicionera* . . . I grabbed another fistful of gravel and put it in my pocket. Then I let the pieces that were still in my hand slide through my fingers one by one.

After a lunch of stewed taters and fried chicken with Nana's runny mojo, Tío Ovi came home from town. On his way to his doctor's appointment he'd got me a planner for when school started up again, which was any minute now, in no time at all, and I still hadn't even filled half my summer-break note-book, though I couldn't care less. I pictured Isora's coloured-in notebook scrawled with arrowed hearts and those ugly blue eyes that looked like buttholes with faces, and then imagined the two of us laughing together. Me and Nana watched the telenovela and my thigh itched from all the jaggedy bits of gravel in my pocket. I stretched out my knee, pressing the gravel harder into my thigh so that the pain would drive me crazy, just as crazy as I was being driven by all the time left until I got to see Isora again.

I spent all day curled up with the Pokémons, taking **BIRDBRAIN** in and out of the grass, battling and battling the Ratikats and doing laps round the gym for no reason while I thought about how I'd wake up bright and early the next morning to see Isora. Me and Nana were tucked in by nine. One of the mattress springs poked out, and my back hurt as badly as the fact that Isora hadn't invited me to the beach with her and that she hadn't called yet to tell me how it went, and I rolled this way and that over the metal until it stung, until my bones hurt so much I thought they'd snap. I woke up from my dreams and heard Ma and Dad when they came back from working in the South. Normally they had a bite of papaya or a ham and cheese sarnie before they went to bed, but that night they went straight to sleep.

The sun was still coming up when I got out of Nana's bed. Ma had left me two euros on the nightstand for chewing gum. I grabbed the money, a roll of bread and a banana and tore down the road. The minimarket was closed. Two old women stood outside whispering and looking around like they were scared. Sinson was on a quilt bed by the back door, snoring so loud it put the fear of God in you, as Nana said. I knocked once, twice, three, five, ten times, but no one let me in. I sat on the front steps. Ayoze and Mencey walked up the road with a football, and I stared down at my two-euro coin so that they wouldn't talk to me. I bent my knee once, twice, six times to make the gravel still jangling in my pocket stab my skin. Ayoze whispered something to Mencey and then elbowed him in the arm, and they kept turning to look at me as they drew further and further away.

Sinson came out front and lay down on top of my knees. Another hour passed. Two. Three. I bent my leg. The gravel in my pocket felt like nails. Whenever a car drove past, Sinson got up, barked after it, then flopped back down in my lap. I heard the sound of tired feet shuffling towards me from far away. It was Eufrasia, heading back from church, a neon-yellow rosary in her hand. Ay, miniña, the shame, you go on home to your nana's. These two won't be back till nightfall. What a cryin' shame, miniña. Such a good girl, and so young too, and Sinson jumped up on her legs. And the two of you were like sisters. You've not got nobody else, have you, no brothers or sisters, you're all alone, aren't you. What a shame it is, Christ almighty, and then Sinson peed on her. Ay, sweet Jesus what a cryin' shame, she said like she was drowning. You tell your mama to start tryin' for a brother, kay? Ay, miniña, I'm always tellin' my kids that the ocean's the devil, and they go on into the water like there's not a danger in the world, jumpin' off cliffs and all the rest of it. Ay miniña, what a cryin' shame it is. Then the old woman took my hand and placed her rosary in the palm, and said, now you go and pray to the Lord Our Father, who's always got our backs. Scat, Sinson, scat, she said as she walked up the road.

I sat there, on the front steps of the minimarket. I closed my hand and looked through a hole at the rosary glowing in the dark. My hand started shaking like crazy and I wasn't sure why. I rushed up the road towards Nana's and my chest started to hurt like somebody'd swung a machete right into me. I got to where Nana's cousin lived and there was nobody outside, no one weeding or spraying pests or digging taters. Somewhere, a goat kid cried. The clouds sped down the side of El Amparo. A gust of cat poop blew towards me from the fields. I stopped in my tracks. My heart beat so hard I thought I'd split in two. I turned round and glanced at the ocean and the sky. The ocean and the sky, which always looked like one great big thing. Instead of continuing up the road, I walked down through the neighbourhood. I went by Nana's cousin's again, and then by the gayhouse, and by Melva's and Conchi's, until I was back at the minimarket. Sinson leaped off the front steps and followed me. I carried on past the cultural centre, and it was closed too. Gaspa, who'd been pissing in a corner by Bar de Antonio, joined Sinson. The bar was empty as well. We walked past the church. Colourful papers fluttered over the square. They looked lovelier than ever as they sparkled and shivered in the air like small, frightened people. Blue yellow white, blue yellow white. We reached Doña Carmen's house and out came her yappy old mutt. He barked at us. I carried on down. I could hear the dogs padding behind me like a procession, clipclipclip. They trailed me just like they had on the day of Isora's cake. But my hands were empty. Eufrasia's rosary had gone missing and I didn't know where or how, maybe I'd tossed it without realizing. One neighbourhood house after another was left behind. I'd never gone this far before. Up front, way down there, the September sun lit everything up. The first light shot through the clouds like a knife dropped from above. We passed a house with old paddocks filled with monks cress, the ones with the fake-looking orange flowers. There was no more mist and no more rain and no more grey clouds, just the sun striking my forehead. I looked behind me. I saw the neighbourhood under a thick donkey-belly of fog. The vulcano peak loomed behind the belfry. We kept walking. Two hours passed, then three. Everything was bright and hot and the beach was in sight.

The dogs barked.

The sun cleaved the rocks.

Acknowledgements

I wish to thank all the people who made this book possible and who accompanied me during its writing. Especially my Spanish editor, Sabina Urraca, for trusting me. Thanks to my father (who always helps me find the words), my mother, my grandmother and my whole jarrapienta family. Thanks to Elisa Victoria, Aida González Rossi, Tara, Héctor, Amanda, Alicia and all my other friends (I love you, chicas). Thanks to Luis for reading and listening to me. Thanks to Editorial Barrett, my publisher in Spain, and to all my international editors. Thanks to my editor in the US, Deborah Ghim, and to the entire Astra House team, and to my UK editor, Lettice Franklin, and the rest of the staff at Weidenfeld & Nicolson. Thanks to Marina Penalva and Casanovas & Lynch for allowing *Dogs of Summer* to cross so many seas and languages. Infinite thanks to my Super Translator Julia Sanches, and to all of my translators, you form a beautiful community of rewriters of this book.